THE DARK ASSASSIN

THE DARK ASSASSIN

JOSEPH DELANEY

GREENWILLOW BOOKS
An Imprint of HarperCollins*Publishers*

HarperCollins Publishers
Since 1817

This book is a work of fiction. References to real people, events, establishments, organizations, or locales are intended only to provide a sense of authenticity, and are used to advance the fictional narrative. All other characters, and all incidents and dialogue, are drawn from the author's imagination and are not to be construed as real.

First published in 2017 in Great Britain by The Bodley Head, an imprint of Random House Children's Books, under the title The Starblade Chronicles: *Dark Assassin.*
First published in 2017 in the United States by Greenwillow Books.

 Printed in the United States of America. For information address HarperCollins Children's Books, a division of HarperCollins Publishers, 195 Broadway, New York, NY 10007.
www.epicreads.com

The text of this book is set in 12-point Venetian 301 BT.
Book design by Paul Zakris

Library of Congress Control Number: 2017950745

ISBN 978-0-06-233459-6 (hardback)

17 18 19 20 21 PC/LSCH 10 9 8 7 6 5 4 3 2 1

Greenwillow Books

FOR MARIE

Do not think that you will be returned to Earth with a beating heart and warm blood coursing through your veins. You will never again dine on fish or meat or berries. Nor will you sip cool water from mountain streams or feel the warmth of the sun on your skin. At first, each return to Earth will be extremely painful, and you may only dwell there during the hours of darkness. Before the cock crows, you must return to the dark, or else be burned to ashes by the first rays of the morning sun.

—HECATE, QUEEN OF THE WITCHES

PROLOGUE

I awoke in darkness, shivering with cold, my mind numb and void of memories.

Who am I?

I was lying on my back, staring up at a pitch-black, starless sky. The full moon hung low on the horizon, and it was the color of blood.

I felt bewildered.

Where am I? I wondered.

I sat up slowly and looked around. The ground was flat, dotted with dead trees and patches of scrub. I could see lights in the distance, and the faint outline of what looked like cottages.

I began to stumble toward them, weak and unsteady on my feet. Perhaps someone there could help me, or at least tell me the name of this strange place. I didn't like the look of that moon; it should have been a pale silvery yellow—not a monstrous bloated thing, its staring face covered in blood. It seemed to be watching every step I took.

I gradually grew stronger and made better progress toward the cottages—but suddenly I was brought to a halt by what sounded like the growl of an animal in the darkness behind me. It growled again, and my anxiety became a stab of fear.

Something was stalking me. I could hear it padding closer in the darkness. Filled with panic, I fled, sprinting toward the nearest of those lights.

I hadn't run far when I saw the silhouette of a figure approaching, walking directly toward me. Now there was danger ahead as well as behind.

I am skilled at judging people by their gait. The figure had a swagger that comes from confidence and walked the walk of a fighter. The threat was growing.

Whoever it was halted about six feet from me; I halted too, my whole body shaking with fear. Perhaps this was the moment when my life ended. Maybe the trembling of my limbs was telling me that my demise was near. . . . My mind was bewildered, but perhaps my body sensed its demise?

"Grimalkin? Is that you?" the figure cried.

The sound of that name acted like a spell. It affected

me profoundly. My body stopped trembling, and my fear fell from my shoulders like a worn-out cloak. Somewhere in the distant past I had heard that name before. I struggled to recall everything that was associated with it.

Then I realized that the voice I'd heard was that of a girl. She stepped closer and smiled; a smile that was like a light illuminating the darkness.

I knew this girl well. Her name was Thorne.

Suddenly the name Grimalkin awoke my memories. Images flashed into my mind in vivid color. I saw my opponents fall before me, their bodies soaked in blood. My knives sliced and pierced; I drew my scissors from the secret sheath beneath my left armpit and snipped away the pallid thumbs of my dead enemies.

Suddenly my identity surged back.

I am Grimalkin.

I am dead. . . .

But I am still Grimalkin.

I was now in the dark. I remembered the confrontation up on Anglezarke Moor. I remembered how I had attacked Golgoth, the Lord of Winter, running toward him with my blades. I'd known that I could not win, but I'd bought time so that Alice, the earth witch, could fight back.

There had been a moment of freezing cold and intense

pain; then I had fallen into the dark. My life as a witch assassin on Earth was over.

My fear ceased. I was now aware of the straps that crisscrossed my body, and was pleased to find my blades in place: short ones for throwing and long ones for fighting at close quarters. I felt under my left armpit: my snippy scissors were also safe in their sheath. There would be other dead witches here in the dark—enemies I had encountered in the past, and perhaps new adversaries too. Would I be able to take their thumb bones to increase my own strength? Was the dark like Earth in some respects?

All at once I was aware that my heart was beating and I was breathing steadily, just as I had on Earth.

It was then that I had a moment of regret.

Never again would I be the witch assassin of the Malkin clan. Another would take my place—probably already had. Nor would I be able to help the humans in their fight against the Kobalos, a race that had waged war, intending to slay all human males and enslave the females. I thought of the girls and women who were already slaves of the Kobalos and felt sad. I had sworn to free them—but now, in the dark, I could no longer keep that vow. I could only hope that my allies left behind on Earth would still prove victorious without my help.

Death was final. It was hard to accept that, but what had happened could not be changed. I had to let the past go and deal with my new situation.

How would things differ now? I wondered. What opportunities would the dark present?

My attention returned to the girl in front of me. When we had known each other, I'd been training her to become a witch assassin like me. We had been close.

I'd wept when my enemies slayed Thorne—but tears are a waste of time. They achieve nothing. And afterward I'd taken my revenge and hunted down every one of her killers.

I glanced at her hands. She had died when her thumbs were sliced away, but now they were whole again.

"It's good to see you, child," I told her.

My memory had now fully returned. My mind was sharp and clear, just as it had been when I was alive—maybe even better.

"It's good to see you again, Grimalkin," Thorne replied. "But I wish we were meeting under better circumstances. The dark's a terrible place. It's hard to survive."

"But you *have* survived, child. I'm impressed," I told her. "I obviously trained you well. Now you can teach me what I need to know of this place."

"That's why I came. When a soul arrives here, the first

hours are the most dangerous. I'll help you, if you will allow it," she said.

"How did you know that I had died?" I asked her.

"There are those here who specialize in knowing the affairs of Earth—we call them Watchers; they take the shape of ravens. They told me of your death, so I came to help you. This dank field is where most of those who serve the dark materialize after death."

"Do you know what happened immediately after my death? Did the others survive?" I asked.

"Yes, I do know much of what happened. Tom Ward and his apprentice, Jenny, continue the struggle against your enemies. The god Pan fought Golgoth and drove him away. But although Pan won that battle, he's badly weakened, and the conflict simmers on. Golgoth will eventually return, stronger and more dangerous than ever. Since then the Kobalos have won battle after battle and are now close to the shores of the Northern Sea. No doubt they plan more attacks upon the County. But there is nothing we can do about it from the dark."

"Thank you for that information," I said.

"We must leave this place immediately," Thorne said, her eyes flickering to and fro as if searching the darkness for some threat. "It is dangerous to remain in one place for too long."

"I put myself in your hands. Lead the way!" I commanded with a smile.

Now the trainee would train her trainer. I followed Thorne toward the distant lights.

As we set off, I glanced back over my shoulder but could see nothing.

"Something was following me," I told Thorne. "It padded on four legs. I was being stalked."

"You'll have to get used to that," she replied. "There are lots of predators in the dark. Some are human, but there are all manner of other creatures that are hungry for blood. They usually concentrate on lone victims; now that there are two of us, we will be more secure. You will find that those who dwell in the dark have formed groups—there is safety in numbers."

We left the wasteland behind and emerged onto a narrow cobbled street. At first glance, it could have been somewhere in the County—Priestown or Caster, perhaps.

The baleful blood moon lit only one half of it, but I could see that the cobbles were a shiny black. On our left was an open drain, with dark, old blood trickling along it. It could have come from a slaughterhouse or a butcher's shop . . . but I sniffed and knew instantly that the blood hadn't come from animals.

It was human blood, its coppery taint clear in the damp air.

On either side of us, the small windows of the houses were illuminated by candlelight, shaded by black lace curtains that twitched like spiderwebs.

Were eyes peering from behind those curtains? I felt sure that they were. If so, were they spies, dead humans, witches, or other creatures of the dark?

Dead people shuffled along the street toward us. Some showed evidence of the manner of their death. A man was staggering forward with a wide gash in his throat that gaped like an extra mouth; he was moaning with pain, and the wound was still dribbling blood.

If you were carried over into this dark domain of the dead complete with your wounds, then I should surely be in bloody fragments—after all, I'd been blasted into pieces of flesh and bone by Golgoth, the Butcher God.

I glanced sideways at Thorne. Why did she still have her thumbs? I wondered. Why was I whole? There was much to learn here. I lived for challenges; I thrived on combat. This was a whole new world to understand and eventually dominate. My interest was roused. Death might even be better than life!

Then I noticed that the dead were walking along with

their eyes fixed on the cobbles, as if they dared not look others in the eye.

"Why do they walk with their eyes cast down?" I asked Thorne.

"So as not to draw attention to themselves," she explained. "These are weak souls who are mostly just prey."

"Prey to what?" I asked.

But before Thorne could answer, I heard a screech in the distance, and simultaneously a big bell began to boom; a terrible tolling that vibrated through the soles of my feet.

Was it some kind of warning? I started to count the peals.

Thorne looked anxious. She pointed toward a narrow alley and started running. I followed her into the shadows. At the thirteenth peal, the tolling stopped. In the new silence I heard screams and wails of terror from every direction.

"What is happening?" I demanded.

"That bell serves more than one purpose," Thorne told me, "but right now it signals an immediate threat. Now predators are permitted to hunt whoever they like. It's best to hide until a single chime signals that the period of danger is over. Predators are legion and take many forms. Look! There's one above us now!" She pointed upward.

Something large swooped low over the alley, letting out a raucous screech. It hovered directly above our heads, bathed in the light of the blood moon. It looked like a giant bat, with glowing eyes and long, bone-tipped wings terminating in clawed hands.

"It's a chyke—one of the lesser demons. They hunt in packs, and we're their chosen prey!" cried Thorne. "They are very sensitive to the fresh blood of new arrivals to the dark. That is why it's found you so quickly! It will be directing other predators toward us. Hopefully the second bell will chime soon."

Anger flared within me. It was not my way to cower in an alley like this, hoping for a bell to save me. I listened carefully. There were cries of fear and pain all around us, but they seemed to be concentrated ahead of us, in the direction of the moon, where they were accompanied by screams of agony. That was where most of the predators and victims must be gathered.

I turned, gestured that Thorne should follow me, and began to run toward that baleful red moon, toward those cries.

"No!" Thorne's voice shook. "That leads to the basilica square. That's the killing ground!"

I ignored her, gathering speed as I ran through the narrow streets, each turn taking me closer to those terrible screams. I could hear Thorne running close at my heels.

"Please, Grimalkin, listen to me!" she called. "There are too many of them to fight. They'll rip us to pieces. You can die again in the dark. And if you do, you become nothing. You fall into oblivion!"

"Better to be nothing than to cringe in fear!" I retorted.

Now I was sprinting, easing the first of my blades out of its leather sheath. The square was a vast flagged area with the great stone walls of the basilica rising up beyond it, even higher than those of Priestown Cathedral.

Who prayed within those walls? To which dark entities did they offer worship?

In front of the basilica, the square was a scene of carnage. The flags ran with blood, and there were bodies everywhere, some dead, others still twitching or attempting to crawl to safety. The air was full of chykes that swooped and tore, slaying those who cowered below. The sound of screams rent the air, but loudest of all was the infernal beating of huge wings.

One creature saw me and glided forward, eyes glowing, talons outstretched. I hurled a blade into its throat and it fluttered to the ground, blood spraying from its open mouth.

Then I raised two of my long blades high above my head and yelled out a challenge: "Here I am! Attack me if you dare!"

Out of the corner of my eye I saw Thorne's face; it was full of alarm and fear. Had the dark diminished her so much? I wondered sadly.

The chykes flocked to where I was standing, and soon I was spinning and whirling, performing my dance of death, slaying my enemies with each stab and thrust of my blades.

Suddenly I realized that the alarm on Thorne's face had changed to grim determination. Soon we were fighting back to back. I laughed as we slew our enemies.

I had gone to the dark, but nothing had changed.

I was still Grimalkin.

Thomas Ward

I
Spook's Business

I accompanied Alice to the edge of the garden, where we halted and kissed good-bye.

"Take care," I begged her. "I don't know what I'd do without you."

Alice was just about the prettiest girl I'd ever seen, but now there was sadness in her beautiful eyes. She felt the same way as I did; we didn't want to be apart.

She was off to Pendle once more to try to form an alliance with the witches there. She'd already made two failed attempts. The three main clans—the Malkins, the Deanes, and the Mouldheels—didn't get along. Well, that was to seriously understate the situation. There was rivalry and hatred between them; sometimes they even fought and killed one another. But an alliance between these clans and our allies was vital if we were to defend the County against the magic of the Kobalos mages.

The witch clans had formed alliances before, so I knew it was possible, and Alice was optimistic. I had to hope.

The dark army of the bestial Kobalos was approaching the far shore of the Northern Sea, their malicious gaze fixed upon our own country. But there was an even more immediate danger. Using powerful magic, their high mages were able to project themselves directly into the County. They could bring a few warriors with them and attack at any time.

By now the military were aware of the army, and the County was on a war footing against the threat of invasion. Forces from the two main barracks, at Burnley and Colne, had marched east to fortify the border. Those that remained were stretched thin, fighting off Kobalos raids. People were scared, and travel was dangerous.

The Kobalos mages had also tried to summon Golgoth, the Lord of Winter, into the County. Had they succeeded, we would have been plunged into a permanent winter, the countryside left frozen and weakened by famine. Only with the help of the Old God Pan, and Alice's powerful magic, had we managed to prevent that. Despite this, I'd never felt so vulnerable; never felt less able to do my duty and protect the County from the dark.

"You take care too, Tom. Ain't going to be away for

more than a week, I promise you," Alice told me now.

We hugged, kissed again, and then she set off for Pendle. She was wearing a green dress and a short brown jacket as protection against the chill air. It was early spring, but as yet there was little warmth in the sun. As she walked away, I glanced down at her pointy shoes, the mark of a witch. Alice had finally gone to the dark, but she wasn't a witch who practiced bone, blood, or familiar magic—she was an earth witch, perhaps the first one ever. She served Pan and drew her magic from the Earth itself.

Just before she reached the edge of the slope, she turned and waved to me. I waved back, and then she was out of sight. Already missing her, I turned back to the garden and headed for the practice post.

As I did so, I saw a silver chain falling toward it, spinning widdershins—against the clock. It formed a spiral, tightening upon the post in the classic manner, achieving a perfect spread from top to bottom. Had that post been a witch, she would have been bound from head to knee, the chain tightening hard against her teeth to prevent her from chanting spells.

"Well done, Jenny!" I called out.

Jenny was my apprentice. I knew that my own master, John Gregory, would never have taken her on. To become a spook's apprentice, you had to be a seventh son of a seventh son.

Jenny was a girl; as far as I knew, she was the first girl ever to have been trained by a spook. She claimed to be a seventh daughter of a seventh daughter, but I'd never been able to verify that, because she'd been brought up by foster parents. Still, I could not deny that she had gifts that were useful when fighting the dark—different ones than mine. She could make herself almost invisible and possessed such great empathy that she could almost read people's minds.

I looked at her as she stood there smiling. Her face was freckled and she had different-colored eyes—the left was blue, the right one brown.

"Well, what's your score?" I demanded.

"I've managed fifteen successes in twenty attempts! A couple more weeks of this and I'll be better than you!" she said cheekily.

That success rate was good, but I would have preferred a little more respect from my apprentice. The trouble was, I was only two years older than her; in August I'd be eighteen and she'd be sixteen. We even shared the same birthday—the third. My own apprenticeship had come to a premature end when my master had been killed fighting enemy witches.

Suddenly a sound drew our attention. It was the pealing of the bell at the withy trees crossroads. Our garden was guarded by the boggart Kratch, which meant that it was dangerous for outsiders to venture in, so those in need of help stayed clear; they usually went to the crossroads and summoned me by ringing the bell.

"It's spook's business," I said softly.

The last couple of days had been quiet, but I'd known that it couldn't last. There were always local threats from the dark in the County. This time the danger might come from the Kobalos.

"Can I come with you?" Jenny asked.

"No, Jenny, it's best that I go alone. You carry on practicing here. You'll need to work a lot harder if you want to be as good as me!"

Here in the garden, the boggart would keep her safe against most things, I knew. Beyond its boundaries, it was a different matter.

I was carrying my staff, but I also had the powerful Starblade in a scabbard on my back. As long as I held it or had it on my person, dark magic couldn't harm me.

"But if it means a journey, can I go with you to sort out the problem?" Jenny persisted.

My apprentice had to be trained, and that meant sharing the danger of our craft. So I nodded, and with a grin, she went to retrieve my silver chain and prepared to cast it at the post again. I supposed that I had to let her learn, just as I had. . . .

As I strode out of the garden and headed toward the sound of that pealing bell, a wave of sadness washed over me. Things had changed so much since I'd begun my own apprenticeship. Not only was my master, John Gregory, dead; Grimalkin, the assassin of the Malkin clan, had been slain by Golgoth. Although she was a witch, she'd been a strong and powerful ally who had taken the lead in fighting the Kobalos. I would almost go so far as to say that she had become a friend. She'd certainly saved my life on several occasions. It was Grimalkin who had forged the Starblade for me, and then trained me in its use. She would be greatly missed.

As I walked, I glanced up at the fells that rose far above the village—Parlick Pike and Wolf Fell. Their summits were still white with snow that sparkled in the sunlight.

As I reached the withy trees, the pealing of the bell ceased. Whoever was ringing it must have heard my approach. People were often nervous when waiting to speak to a spook, not sure what to expect from the man who wore a cloak and carried a staff and a silver chain. Sometimes those nerves got the better of them and they left before I arrived.

I headed into the shade of the trees and saw a stocky figure standing by the bell rope, which was dancing and swaying at his side. He wore a black gown and hood and even carried a staff—he was dressed like a spook! Who could it be? This man was surely too broad to be Judd Brinscall, who worked the territory north of Caster.

I halted close to him, and he suddenly pulled back his hood to reveal his face.

The shock of what I saw took my breath away.

It was impossible.

I was gazing at a dead man.

2

Training a Girl

Bill Arkwright had died in Greece fighting a rear-guard action against the dangerous fire elementals that had pursued us. He'd taken up a position between us and their deadly flames, thus buying time, but sacrificing his life so that the Spook, Alice, and I could escape.

In appearance, this was certainly the Arkwright I remembered—the man who, at the request of John Gregory, had given me six months' training to toughen me up.

He had a shaved head, striking green eyes, and a sturdy body that suggested great strength. The rowan staff he carried differed from mine, which had a retractable blade; his was tipped with a twelve-inch blade with six backward-facing barbs, three on each side. By his side lay a heavy bag at least twice the size of the one I usually carried.

Yes, this was the exact likeness of the Bill Arkwright I remembered from life. I had once encountered what I thought was Arkwright's ghost, its face badly burned, as if by a fire elemental, but the man who stood before me had no scars whatsoever.

Instantly I was on my guard. This could be a trick. Kobalos high mages were expert shape-shifters.

I cast my staff down on the ground and drew the Starblade from its scabbard, gripping it with both hands and pointing it at the figure before me

"Throw down your staff and kneel on your hands!" I commanded.

"Well, Master Ward, what sort of a welcome do you call this?" the figure growled angrily, sounding just like Bill Arkwright. "I've traveled a long way to greet you, and what do I get for my pains? I'm threatened with a rusty sword!"

"It's the only welcome you'll get until I'm sure you're who you say you are," I retorted.

The Starblade wasn't much to look at, I knew, but it was incredibly sharp and strong. If I wielded it with confidence, it could slice through the toughest armor. It would also defend me against any dark magic that might be used against me here. The witch assassin Grimalkin had imbued it with her powerful magic.

Rather than obeying my command, the man held his staff at an angle of forty-five degrees, in the defensive position. Then he sucked in a breath and suddenly attacked, bringing the weapon round in an arc, aiming at my head.

But suspicion had made me ready. I raised the Starblade to block the blow, and with barely a shudder, the sword cut into his staff as if it was butter, slicing it neatly in two. I paused, not pressing home my attack. Arkwright had taken aim with the base of his staff rather than the blade, so he hadn't intended to kill me.

He threw the two pieces of staff away in disgust and glared at me.

"I'll tell you just one more time. Kneel on your hands!" I shouted angrily.

"Well, Master Ward, I'm prepared to humor you for a while. But if you know what's good for you, you won't try my patience too far."

The man who called himself Bill Arkwright slowly knelt down on the ground, glaring up at me sullenly, his hands at his sides.

"Now kneel on your hands!" I ordered.

For a moment I thought he was going to refuse, but then, with a scowl, he did so.

"We have a problem," I told him. "I believed you to be

dead, slain in Greece years ago. If you survived, then why wait so long to come here and show yourself?"

"You have the gifts of a seventh son of a seventh son," he said calmly. "What about that sense of cold that tells you something from the dark is close by? Do you feel it now? If you don't, I'm *not* from the dark, and well you know it!"

From somewhere to my left, in the shadows of the trees, came the raucous cry of a raven. I forced myself not to be distracted, despite the racket it was making. I focused all my attention on the figure kneeling on his hands.

I shook my head.

"Then I'm not from the dark—it's as simple as that!" Arkwright insisted.

I thought back. . . . I had never actually seen his dead body in Greece.

"Nothing is simple anymore," I told this man. "Many times I've been close to the dark and never had that warning. It doesn't always work, especially with the powerful Kobalos mages. *You* could be one of them." I'd already encountered a human who'd turned out to be one of the high mages—second in rank and power only to the triumvirate that ruled the Kobalos.

"Then we have a standoff, Master Ward. So how can

we resolve it?" Arkwright asked me.

"Let's start with some explanations from you. How did you survive the encounter with the fire elementals? Then, assuming you did so, why did it take you so long to return here? The help of another spook would have been useful over the past years. So where were you when you were needed?"

"I was badly hurt when I fought those demonic elementals to give *you* time to escape," Arkwright said angrily. "For a while I lost my sight, but the damage was more to my mind than my body. I wandered in Greece for a long time, not caring if I lived or died. I begged like a dog. . . . I turned to drink again. You remember that old weakness of mine, Master Ward?"

I nodded. Bill Arkwright had been addicted to red wine, but he'd overcome his need. It was plausible that he'd lapsed into his old ways. Many people addicted to alcohol did exactly that.

"It took me a long time to kick the habit and find myself again. But at last I did, and I embarked on the long sea voyage from Greece. There were rumors of war—a threat from the north—but little hard information was to be had. When I reached the County, I learned that John Gregory was dead and that his apprentice, Tom Ward, was the new Chipenden Spook. So I'm here to offer my services. Better late than never, eh?"

"If you really *are* Bill Arkwright, your help will be very welcome. But I have to be sure. You wouldn't believe the things I've seen and experienced, the deceits that have been perpetrated."

I had been the pawn of others too many times. For all I knew, I could be confronting Balkai, the most powerful of the Kobalos mages, in human form. His magic couldn't harm me while I had the Starblade, but I had to be vigilant. How could I ever be certain that this was indeed Bill Arkwright?

As I reached forward and tugged the bell rope, I heard the beating of wings: the raven had taken flight. I hoped that Jenny would hear the ringing bell and, knowing that I was already at the crossroads, come and investigate. Maybe her gift of empathy could help me get at the truth.

"Who are you calling?" Arkwright asked me, looking up at the bell swinging above us.

"Jenny, my apprentice."

"Did I hear you correctly, Master Ward? Your apprentice is called Jenny? You're training a *girl*?"

3
Little Cat

We stood glaring at each other in silence until I heard Jenny approaching through the trees.

She walked quickly toward us, a figure full of youthful energy. But when she noticed my prisoner kneeling on his hands before me, she began to slow down. She came to a halt, her eyes glancing at the two pieces of rowan staff on the ground.

"Is he a spook?" she asked me.

"Perhaps," I answered. "He looks like a spook called Bill Arkwright who once trained me for six months. But I fear that he is really something else. Is he a Kobalos mage?"

There was a silence as Jenny stared at the man in front of us.

"He looks like Arkwright and he talks like Arkwright. But I believed Arkwright to be dead," I went on. "Now, after years away, he turns up out of the blue. He has a plausible story to account for his absence, but we can't afford to take any chances. So you tell me what you think. Use your gift of empathy. Tell me what the inside of his head looks like."

"Empathy!" sneered the man kneeling before us. "So she has gifts like we do, only hers are different. Is that it? Next you'll be telling me that she's the seventh daughter of a seventh daughter!"

"I am!" Jenny moved a little closer to him.

He shifted his weight, so I jabbed the point of the sword toward his throat. "Keep still. I'll assume the slightest move to be a threat!" I warned.

"This may not work," Jenny said uneasily. She frowned, then closed her eyes in concentration. She stood there for a few seconds, then opened her eyes wide and jabbed her finger toward the kneeling man.

"He has a temper! He's very angry with you for doubting him. He likes a drink too. That temptation is always there. He'll never be free of it—there's a lot of pain deep inside him. He's all mixed up, I think. He's dangerous too, with a ruthless streak. He loves dogs, but he hates witches!" she finished, turning to look at me.

"That's a good summary of the Bill Arkwright I knew. But is it really him? Is he human or Kobalos?" I asked.

"Witches and mages are hard to empathize with. He seems human enough to me," Jenny replied.

"But maybe a clever Kobalos mage could shield his mind with the thoughts of someone else," I said, thinking aloud.

"Surely there are some things that such an impersonator wouldn't know," said Arkwright. "We've a lot of history between us, Master Ward. What about the months I spent training you? Ask me a question that only I would know the answer to."

The first question came to mind very quickly: "How did you teach me to swim?" I asked.

"I threw you into the canal! Cold, wasn't it? But it worked!"

I stared at the man and nodded. Then I thought of something that only the real Bill Arkwright could know. He would find this painful, but it had to be done.

"There was something about the mill where you lived that I found really strange. It was a situation that most spooks wouldn't have tolerated," I said, studying him closely.

Pain clouded his eyes, and he let out a deep sigh. "I had ghosts there. Spooks usually rid buildings of any such entities—that's part of their job—but I hadn't. I know you didn't like it, Master Ward, but as you finally discovered, the ghosts were those of my parents, Abe and Amelia. I kept their coffins in their bedroom at the top of the house. My father was killed when he fell from the roof. My mother couldn't bear to live without him, so she threw herself under the waterwheel.

"Because she was a suicide, she couldn't cross to the light, so my father's ghost chose to stay with her so she wouldn't be alone. I'd done my level best to send them to the light, but I failed—as did our master, John Gregory. But it was you, Master Ward, who won their freedom. At great risk to yourself, you made a bargain with the Fiend, and he released my mother. Then they were both able to go to the light. I'll be eternally grateful for that."

I nodded. Only Bill Arkwright could know these details. Surely it had to be him.

Jenny and I exchanged glances, and I nodded. Then I turned back to Arkwright.

"We managed to destroy the Fiend, but now we have a worse enemy," I told him. "I'd be happy to have your help. I'm sorry for doubting you."

I sheathed the Starblade and held out my hand. Bill Arkwright gripped it, and I hauled him to his feet.

The boggart made the breakfasts, but other meals were down to us, and neither Jenny nor I was a particularly good cook. However, Bill Arkwright was—my mouth still watered when I remembered the fish he'd cooked back at the mill—and that evening he served up a delicious chicken casserole.

I still felt a little ill at ease with him, but as we sat eating our supper in the kitchen, I tried to bring him up to date with all that had happened. While we talked, Jenny remained silent, no doubt sensing his attitude toward girl apprentices.

"What happened to my three dogs?" Arkwright asked suddenly.

"Blood and Bone are still alive and well. They're with a spook called Judd Brinscall who's living at the watermill and covering your old territory. But their mother, Claw, is dead," I told him. "She was killed in the same battle as John Gregory."

I was surprised when Arkwright didn't comment on the death of his dog. He simply nodded and said, "They're my dogs and I want them back with me. And I think I'd like to take a look at the mill."

Bill Arkwright had specialized in hunting water witches across the nearby marsh and had used his big wolfhounds to help him in this task.

"Would you want to take over that area again?" I asked him.

"Why not, Master Ward? After all, I worked the area north of Caster for years—I'm an expert at dealing with creatures from the dark that live in water. Even John Gregory deferred to me when we dealt with water witches."

"Judd is a good man—he's settled into your old role now. You left the mill to John Gregory, and when he drew up his own will he left this house and the one at Anglezarke to me, for as long as I should practice the trade of a spook. He gave the use of the watermill to Judd, who now thinks it's his for life."

"But I'm not dead, so that part of the will is void, isn't it? Couldn't Judd take over the winter house up on Anglezarke Moor?" Arkwright asked, forking a large piece of chicken into his mouth.

I shrugged. "I suppose he could. It would be good to have three spooks working this part of the County."

"Would you come with me to the mill? It might make things easier. After all, this Brinscall has never met me. I don't think I'd take kindly to someone asking me to kneel on my hands again."

"We could set off tomorrow if you like," I suggested.

Arkwright shook his head. "I've been traveling for weeks, so if you don't mind, I'd like to rest here for a few days first. Besides, there's something that needs doing.

Could you lend me a staff while I sort out a new one?"

"Of course. I always keep a few spares. What is it you plan to do?" I asked.

Arkwright had been ignoring Jenny. Now he fixed his eyes on her for the first time. "I propose to see what this young lady is made of. It seems strange to me, a girl being trained as a spook. It would have troubled John Gregory, as well you know. But you've taken her on and she needs to be able to survive—"

"Don't refer to me as 'she'!" Jenny retorted angrily. "She's the cat's mother!"

"Well, you'll get your chance to pay me back, little cat—that's if you're good enough. Tomorrow I'll give you a taste of what I taught your master. I'll teach you to fight with a staff. So get ready for some whacks and bumps!"

Bill Arkwright was as good as his word. Late the next morning I watched them face each other in the garden, staffs held in the diagonal defensive position, blades retracted.

Jenny looked pale. I suspected that she was scared.

Arkwright's expression was mean. "Let's see what you've got, girl. You attack; I'll defend."

She rushed in and swung her staff at his head. He

blocked it with ease. She tried again, with the same result. Then she backed off and took a deep breath, looking ready to give up—though I knew that my apprentice had more spirit than that.

Fighting with a staff was one aspect of her training that I'd neglected. It had been the same when my own master taught me. He'd given me the basics, but passed me on to Arkwright to learn the fine art of fighting with staffs, and to be toughened up.

Jenny suddenly ran at him, swinging her staff like a maniac, aiming blow after blow. Not one of them landed, despite the speed and fury with which they were delivered. By now she was red in the face, but Arkwright blocked each attack with ease. Then, almost casually, he struck back for the first time, making contact with her left arm, just above the elbow. She gave a cry and dropped her staff.

Bill Arkwright shook his head. "Now you're defenseless. You must never drop your staff, little cat. And there was no need to do so then. I hit your left arm. No doubt it was numb—I probably hit the nerve; that was my intention—and your fingers couldn't maintain their grip. But what about your right hand? I didn't hit that arm, did I? So there was no need to let your staff fall. Never drop it. That weapon might be all that stands between you and death! Even one-handed, it can be wielded with deadly effect. Now pick it up, and we'll try again."

He worked with Jenny for over an hour, correcting her stance and showing her how to feint and deceive an opponent before delivering a surprise blow. But he never struck her on the head; he went a lot easier on her than he had when training me. She might have ended up with a sore arm, but she suffered no other cuts or bruises.

"We might make something of you eventually, Mistress Jenny!" Arkwright said at last, with a grin. "I'll give you another lesson tomorrow. Now, Master Ward, would you mind if I cut myself a length of rowan wood for a replacement staff? This one you loaned me is good enough, but I prefer something larger."

"Help yourself," I told him. "I'm sorry I damaged the other one. There are several rowan trees in the western garden."

Jenny and I watched as he cut a branch and trimmed it. Then he removed the fearsome blade from the broken half of his original staff and bound it into position on the new one.

"I pity the water witch who gets in the way of this!" he said.

Arkwright had been ruthless in his dealing with such denizens of the dark. Unlike John Gregory, who'd put witches in pits indefinitely to keep the County safe, Arkwright had sentenced them to only a year or two underground. Once their sentence was served, he dragged the witch out of the pit and killed her. Then, in order to ensure that she didn't come back from the dead, he would cut out her heart and throw it to his dogs.

"Where is John Gregory's grave?" Arkwright asked suddenly. "Is it by the local churchyard, or did you put him to rest near the Wardstone?"

Priests didn't usually allow a spook to be buried in hallowed ground; their bodies were occasionally blessed but were always laid to rest just outside the perimeter of a cemetery. I'd done what I knew my master would have wished.

"He was brought home. He's buried in the western garden," I said. "Would you like to see his grave?"

Arkwright nodded, and the three of us walked toward it.

"You've put the grave right next to the seat!" he exclaimed.

"It was his favorite spot," I replied.

This was where he had taught his apprentices. It had a great view of the fells rising above the trees. He would pace back and forth, teaching me things spook's business while I sat there taking notes.

Bill Arkwright stared down at the inscription.

Here Lieth
John Gregory of Chipenden,
The Greatest of the County Spooks

"You chose the words yourself, Master Ward?" he asked.

I nodded and caught Jenny's eye. She looked sad. She had never met John Gregory, but she was no doubt picking up those feelings from me.

"You chose well," said Arkwright. "Nothing truer was ever written."

Grimalkin

4
The Safe House

Combat has always absorbed and enthralled me. As I fought the demon chykes on the bloody flags in front of the tall basilica, I lost track of time. The fighting seemed to take place in a timeless present, and I was lost in the joy of combat.

Much to my disappointment, it came to an end with a single peal from the great bell.

The predators immediately took flight, the tumult of their beating wings fading into the distance as they soared over the basilica to leave the sky above us empty. But the cobbles still ran with blood, and more than a dozen chykes lay there, dead or dying.

"I know a place where we could take refuge for a while and talk," Thorne said. "It's a safe house."

I stared at her. "Alice told me that when she was here in the dark, you also took her to a safe house. Is it the same one? The one where you betrayed her?"

Alice had ventured into the dark in order to retrieve the Dolorous Blade, a special weapon that could bring about the destruction of the Fiend. She had been met by Thorne, who had promised to help her.

But Thorne had lied—though she had later saved Alice's life and had more than redeemed herself through her subsequent deeds. I'd intended to show my displeasure, but I felt sure that she could be trusted now.

Thorne looked down, unable to meet my gaze. "Yes," she admitted, "it is the same one. I'm ashamed of what I did. But I hope that Alice told you the full story. . . ."

I nodded. "Yes, I know that after that betrayal, you proved yourself loyal and trustworthy. Take me to this safe house. We have much to discuss."

Soon we were sitting cross-legged, facing each other beside a huge pit of murky water in a gloomy damp cellar—just as Alice had described.

A single torch flickered upon the wall. Thorne had her back to it so that her face was in darkness.

"Do you forgive me for what I did here?" she asked me.

"Alice forgave you. That is enough. But she never explained the reason for your betrayal," I replied.

"I was lonely and afraid. The dark's a terrifying place,

and I'd have done almost anything to escape. But there was something that motivated me even more than fear and misery: my ambition, a dream that I strived to fulfill. I'd hoped to become the greatest witch assassin of the Malkin clan, surpassing even your achievements, Grimalkin. Death had taken that opportunity from me. I was offered a chance to go back to Earth . . . a chance to realize my ambition. For that I betrayed Alice, and I'm truly sorry."

"Put it behind you, child. Alice told me what you did later—how you helped her, how you faced up to the demon Beelzebub and took his thumb bones. But to return to Earth and live one's life again—that is an astonishing thought. Is that possible, or did they lie to you? Can a dead witch *really* leave the dark and live on Earth again?"

Thorne shrugged. "I was promised that by Morwena."

Morwena had been the most powerful of the water witches. With the help of Tom Ward, I'd defeated her and sent her soul into the dark.

"Alice said that Morwena was slain here," I said.

"Yes, she was slain for a second time here in the dark. A skelt stabbed her with its bone tube—it went right through her neck and emerged from her mouth. Then it drained her of blood. Now she's ceased to exist. That is the danger that faces all of us here."

"Did Morwena say how your return to life would be accomplished? Did she herself possess such powerful magic?" I asked.

Thorne shook her head. "Morwena was strong, but even she couldn't have managed that. Only the power of the Old Gods could achieve it. That's what she told me, anyway. She said that it was only possible if two such gods, working together, willed it."

"Which of the Old Gods would she have invoked?"

"She didn't say, but I assume that the Fiend was one of them. I was a fool to listen to her. Even if it were possible, she'd never have kept her promise," Thorne said, shaking her head.

"But what if it *is* possible, child? What if we could be returned to Earth?"

"I'd love to go back too. I feel that I was cheated of my life."

"Then perhaps we could both return. If I made it possible, would you fight against our enemies alongside me?"

"Of course I would. But how would we accomplish that?" Thorne asked.

"I can think of one god who might help—Pan," I replied.

Pan was the enemy of Talkus, the god of the Kobalos, and his ally Golgoth. Pan might be willing to help me. But first I had to find him.

"Do you know where in the dark the domain of Pan is?" I asked Thorne.

"The domains are constantly shifting. They never stay in one place for long. But given time, I could find it. First we'd have to find a way out of this domain. There's just one gate, but it's not always in the same location. At the moment, it's somewhere inside the basilica. It gives off a faint maroon light, which is much easier to see in the dark. Then there's the smell; it stinks of rotten eggs. No, there'll be no problem finding that gate, but I've enemies there—Bony Lizzie, for one, and of course Beelzebub will be seeking revenge too."

"What exactly do we face? Who else was present when you took his bones?" I wanted to know.

"Tusk, the abhuman, was there. He's strong and very dangerous, but I stabbed him through the forehead with my scissors, and he is no more," Thorne told me. "Old Mother Malkin was with Lizzie, but I don't see her as a threat. I forgot . . . there's another thing you need to know: magic doesn't work inside the basilica. If it did, Beelzebub would have blasted me before I could get anywhere near him. But he does have some abilities that transcend magic—they're part of him, and he used them to control the gate. Despite the loss of his thumb bones, he might still do so. He and Lizzie will be the main threats we face."

"You can leave them to me, child," I said. "If they stand in our way, they'll wish they hadn't. All you need to worry about is getting me to that gate so that we can escape from here. But before we go, I'd like to know a few more things about the dark. When we entered this town and walked down that first cobbled street, I saw that some of the dead still bore the wounds that had caused their demise. It's as if they carried them over into the dark. So why am I not reduced to bloody pieces, as I was when Golgoth slayed me? And you—why have you still got your thumb bones, Thorne?"

"When I first came here, I had no thumb bones—it made it hard for me to hold my weapons, let me tell you! Sometimes I even used my toes! But after I took Beelzebub's thumb bones, mine were returned to me. I'm not sure why. And I don't know how you managed to enter the dark in one piece. Maybe Pan will tell you."

I smiled. "That's all the more reason to seek him out, then. But tell me more about these predators. How are things organized here? Is it kill or be killed? How are the prey chosen?"

"They are usually weak souls who select themselves for that role. They are easily taken by the strong. . . . Do you thirst, Grimalkin?" Thorne asked me suddenly.

"Yes," I said. "My mouth is very dry."

"Well, the water here will do nothing but make you vomit. There is only one source of nourishment in the dark, and that's blood. Blood witches would be more at home here—even though, back on Earth, they drink only small amounts of blood during their magic rituals. Here it must be consumed in far greater quantities. On Earth, we bone witches ate the same food as humans and preferred our meat cooked. Here we must drink a lot of blood. At first I found it very difficult."

"Is there no other way?" I asked, wrinkling my nose in disgust at the thought.

Thorne shook her head. "If you don't drink blood, you will become weak and die the second death. It's as simple as that. Blood is also the currency here. It can be obtained in special shops and hostelries, but at a price—weak souls are employed to seek out victims or give information on their whereabouts. The strong don't need to compromise themselves in such a way. They take blood directly from chosen victims. Drink the blood of a strong witch, and you'll acquire her strength."

"Then Lizzie had better not cross my path," I retorted. "If I must drink blood, it might as well be hers!"

5 What Humans Call Hell

Keeping to the shadows as best we could to avoid the glare of the blood moon, Thorne and I returned to the basilica along narrow cobbled streets. The greatest moment of danger was when we crossed the open flagged space to reach the shelter of its walls, but the bell remained silent and the air empty of chykes. I would have liked to kill a few more, but we needed to conserve our strength for what lay ahead.

We climbed the precipitous stone steps that led to a door at the top; the one entrance that Thorne thought wouldn't be guarded or locked—and indeed, she simply pushed it open, and we stepped through into darkness.

"I've been in here before, so I'll lead the way," she said. "There's a spiral staircase leading below ground."

I followed her down the steps, descending widdershins, unable to see anything. There was no dangerous stairwell that we could topple into, but the stairs were steep and narrow, and my shoulders brushed against cold damp stone on either side.

We came out onto a narrow ledge above what might have been a vast natural cavern, but for the statues and carvings on the walls, which were illuminated by torches. The floor was a long way down, and it seemed to me that it must lie considerably lower than the square in front of the basilica.

Thorne pointed downward. "Can you see those altars below?" she asked.

I peered down and saw a number of structures on the distant floor. Some were square; others round or oblong. "Which gods do they honor?" I kept my voice low, but it still echoed faintly from the walls of that huge place.

"Most of the deities from the dark are represented there. One statue—that of the Fiend—has been removed, now that he's ceased to exist. But he had a domain of his own, and it's very close to this one. If we succeed in passing through the gate, that's where we'll end up. Of course there's no danger from him now, but other entities will have taken up residence there. On my last visit I came across skelts."

"Why is there nobody below? Where are the worshippers?"

"Each deity is worshipped at different times . . . though there should certainly be devotees tending the altars."

"So they could be lying in wait for us?" I asked.

"It's a possibility," answered Thorne. "When I came here with Alice, we were ambushed and fell into their hands. That was because Morwena's magic was powerful enough to detect our presence even from a distance. But she's dead now. I don't expect any others will know that we've entered the basilica."

I was not reassured by her words. I didn't like the emptiness of the floor below. Something was wrong. I sensed danger. . . .

We descended a further flight of steps cautiously and emerged onto the floor. I glanced at the nearest altar, where I saw an effigy of Hecate, the so-called Queen of the Witches—although none of the Pendle clans had ever recognized her as such. She was depicted with a regal, imperious smile, but her eyes were cruel. Black lilies were strewn at her feet, filling the cauldron at the base of the plinth. That cauldron was believed to be the source of her power.

Beyond her stood another altar, this time dedicated to Xanatu, the deity of snakes and poisons; he had the body of a man but the head of a serpent. Looking around, I saw that there were more than fifty plinths here, each an altar to a god of the dark. And there, in the distance, right in the center of the chamber, was an empty platform, the largest of them all. This was where the statue of the Fiend had stood; following his destruction, it had been removed.

I wondered again at the absence of worshippers. Surely some should be here, praying to their chosen god.

The chamber was roughly circular, and there were doorways spaced evenly around its circumference—maybe more than a score. All but two were shrouded in darkness.

I led Thorne toward the first of the illuminated openings. As we approached, I heard a dull, rhythmical thudding sound. I drew one of my long blades and peered inside.

There, within the small chamber, was the demon Beelzebub, sitting on a high dais with his back to the wall. Only one candle flickered with yellow light, but it was enough to reveal the situation at a glance. It immediately accounted for that thudding sound. The demon was banging the back of his head against the stone wall.

His face was twisted in agony, but this was not only caused by the banging. Beelzebub was holding out his hands, and the wounds where his thumbs had been dripped of blood. He was experiencing terrible pain and was in no position to threaten us. I glanced at the two large bones on Thorne's necklace. In slicing the thumb bones off his hands, she had reduced him to this pitiful state.

I smiled at her. "You did well, child!" I said.

But there was a second figure in that room—a female—though she scarcely appeared human. Perhaps only a third of the size of a normal adult, she was clothed in a slimy dark dress, and her face was twisted and stretched, almost as if it had been melted and reshaped. Her tongue protruded from her mouth, and her neck was impossibly elongated as it jerked right, then left, right, then left, catching each globule of blood that dripped from Beelzebub's two wounds.

"It's old Mother Malkin!" Thorne exclaimed.

I knew the story of Mother Malkin. She had once been the strongest of the Malkins and had terrorized the County, roaming far and wide, and only rarely returning to Pendle. Tom Ward had clashed with her in the early days of his apprenticeship, knocking her into a river with his staff and drowning her. But she was so strong that she had returned into a rare undead state, soft and malleable, able to ooze into a victim's ears and possess his body.

There are two ways to make sure that a witch cannot return from the dead: burn her or eat her heart. Tom had done neither, but in trying to escape, she had taken refuge in a pigpen at the family farm, and there the huge hungry swine had devoured Mother Malkin for him. As a consequence, she had been hurled into the dark, where she was trapped for all eternity.

As I watched, the demon's blood suddenly ceased dripping—though he continued to hit his head against the wall. Now I could hear two other sounds: his whimpers of pain and the buzzing of the flies above him. Now I remembered that one of Beelzebub's titles was the Lord of the Flies.

Old Mother Malkin looked up, dismayed by the drying up of the blood. She lifted her long gown, which was soaked in the stuff, and sucked greedily at the hem. Neither she nor Beelzebub seemed to be aware of our presence.

Moments later the blood began to drip again, so I put my hand on Thorne's shoulder and led her away.

"The gate was here last time, and that demon controlled it," she told me. "Don't think it's here now, though. Don't sense it at all. He can't even control *himself*, can he?" she said, nodding at Beelzebub.

"Then we'll try the next chamber," I said, leaving the room.

"Shouldn't we put them out of their misery?" Thorne asked.

I shook my head. "Let them suffer. They deserve it. For them, the dark has truly become what humans call hell."

I approached the second illuminated doorway with caution. This might hold a real threat. I glanced through, and saw one person in the chamber—a witch who I knew of old.

It was Bony Lizzie, Alice's mother. She was sitting cross-legged on the floor, staring into space.

She looked up as we entered, and the blank expression on her face flickered into life. I had expected to see fear there, but instead I found hope.

There had been no fondness between Lizzie and me, but given that we were from the same clan, perhaps she expected us to help her now. Did she think we would be her new allies? Thorne had told me that in the dark, predators often combined strength, but Lizzie's remaining companions, Beelzebub and Mother Malkin, were now useless to her.

"It's good to see you, Grimalkin," she said, smiling falsely. She looked a little like Alice, and had no doubt once been pretty, but her years as a cruel malevolent witch had shaped her face into a sly caricature.

"Is it good to see me as well?" Thorne challenged. "Last time we met, you attacked me and Alice. No doubt you would've destroyed us both, unnatural mother that you are. But things didn't go as you expected, did they? I took Beelzebub's thumbs and still wear them around my neck. I slew the abhuman Tusk too. Your two remaining allies are in no position to come to your aid. How you are fallen! This is where you belong, so don't seek to greet us in friendship now!"

Lizzie did her best to smile at Thorne, but instead radiated a shifty malice.

I readied myself to repel an attack from the witch. Thorne had told me that dark magic didn't work here, but Lizzie had always been strong and fast, using her fingernails to take someone's sight or slit their throat.

"Stick together, we should, and help each other," she said craftily. "We three be from the same clan, and 'tis a dangerous place here. Can't you forgive the past? What's done is done. We should think ahead. Make plans for our mutual benefit."

I didn't believe a word that came out of her twisted mouth. Thorne's eyes blazed with fury, and she launched herself at Lizzie, blades unsheathed, but I pulled her back. She hissed and struggled for a moment, then stopped when I put my hand on her shoulder and smiled at her. Then I asked Bony Lizzie for information.

"Where are the worshippers? Why are the altars out there abandoned?"

"Everyone's scared—and with good reason," she replied, taking a step back and regarding Thorne warily. "The gods don't respond to sacrifices 'cause there's a big battle coming. It'll decide everything. Some say Talkus will win—he'll make his altar on that big plinth that used to belong to the Fiend. But the gods keep changing their minds about whose side they're on, so the dead stay away. Better to be absent than on the losing side, don't you think?"

"But *you* haven't gone, Lizzie. Why have *you* stayed here?" I asked.

"I've nowhere else to go now. It ain't safe out there. Morwena used to protect me once, but she's gone too, slayed by one of those cursed skelts that serve Talkus."

"We're looking for the gate, Lizzie—the portal to get us out of here. Do you know where it is?"

I watched as a cunning look came into Lizzie's eyes; she clambered to her feet and took a step toward us. "That gate leads to the Fiend's domain. A dangerous place that be, with lots of things fighting one another. Not somewhere anyone with sense would stay. And what about after that? If you found the gate, where would you go then?"

Thorne answered for me. "I know where the second gate is. Then we'd follow the narrow path between domains."

I still had my hand on Thorne's shoulder—I could feel the tension in her body. She was itching to put an end to Lizzie, but I didn't want that; this witch could be useful to us.

"If you take me with you out onto the path, I'll show you where the portal is," Lizzie offered eagerly.

"We'll take you with us, Lizzie, don't you worry. Just show us the path," I agreed.

Thorne glared at me in amazement. No doubt she'd have liked to extract the information by causing Lizzie pain, but this was easier and quicker. If we gave the witch enough rope, she would hang herself. All we had to do was be alert for treachery and deal with her the moment she tripped up.

"Follow me, sisters!" she crowed, and led the way out of the chamber.

Thorne spat after her, just missing her left heel, but I simply smiled and winked.

6
The Demon Tanaki

Bony Lizzie led the way through one of the other dark doorways. We followed a passageway for ten minutes or more, taking the left turn at each fork.

"We're getting near!" said Thorne, wrinkling her nose. "I can smell the gate. We'll be able to see it soon."

She was right. Ahead, in the darkness, I could just make out a very faint maroon glow. Then, as we got nearer, I saw two hoops, each spinning widdershins, against the clock—black and maroon, maroon and black, shifting between those two colors. I could smell it too now . . . a sickening stink of rotten eggs.

It was the gate. Within the circles, another domain was just visible—the one that had once belonged to the Fiend. I could see the inside of a building: flags, stone walls, and what looked like a cauldron.

Beckoning to us, Lizzie headed through the portal;

I noticed that as she dived through, her legs stuck out at odd angles. But despite her awkwardness, she passed through the gate successfully.

"I'll go next, in case Lizzie's planning some sort of treachery," I said, and dived through the spinning hoop, landing on hard flags before coming to my feet in front of Lizzie, who was moaning and rubbing her skinned knees. Thorne appeared just a second later, and I began to take stock of my surroundings.

We were in a large kitchen full of cauldrons, pans, and cooking utensils. It seemed to be deserted.

"This is part of a huge castle," Thorne said. "We've a long walk ahead of us, but I know the way to the next gate—the one that will take us out onto the path between domains."

So, with Thorne in the lead and me bringing up the rear so that I could keep an eye on Lizzie, we set off. Thorne certainly hadn't exaggerated the distance, but she knew where she was going. After descending three flights of stairs to a covered courtyard, we were faced with a choice of three passages. Without hesitation she led us along the central one.

After some time, we came to the edge of a vast dark gray lake and followed a narrow path bounded by a curved stone wall along its shore. We hadn't emerged into the open air. Again there was rock not too far above our heads.

"Everything in this domain is underground," she said, pointing upward. "There is no sky—it makes me feel uncomfortable, as if there's a great weight above about to fall and squash me. Here, the biggest risk we face is skelts. I discovered the danger when I was with Alice," Thorne continued. "They're probably still around. This was the Fiend's domain, but no doubt the servants of Talkus occupy it now."

"There'll be worse things here than skelts," Lizzie said with a cackling laugh. "Let's hope we don't meet one of them."

I didn't comment. It seemed to me that Thorne was more likely to be right. Skelts lurked near water and might well be hiding beneath the surface of the lake.

As we walked, the roof of rock receded until it was much higher, and on our left was a huge cliff, within it a dark, cavelike entrance.

"Through there is the Fiend's throne room; that's where we killed Raknid, the spider demon," Thorne said. "We haven't far to go now. Last time we searched for hours, but now I know exactly where the gate is."

I looked closer, but said nothing. I saw that what I'd thought was a cave was actually a doorway in the outer wall of some huge building. We entered and turned into a narrow passageway. Thorne led us at a rapid pace. She seemed confident, but I just hoped that the gate hadn't moved.

My fears were groundless. Soon I saw it ahead—the same faint maroon glow, the two spinning hoops—and smelled the stink of rotten eggs. We went through as last time, emerging onto a white path that floated off into the darkness. Above was a sky without stars. I glanced over the edge and saw an abyss dropping away below us.

I gestured ahead. "Is that the way to Pan's domain?"

Thorne shrugged. "We've reached the path, and that's the most important step. It doesn't matter which direction we take now; forward or back, this will eventually lead us where we want to go. It may take some time, and will involve passing through many other domains. Nothing is certain, because domains shift relative to one another. If we're lucky, Pan's domain could be the first we come across."

So we set off along the white path in the direction we were facing, with Thorne in the lead. Once again I walked behind Lizzie; I didn't trust her. Surely, I thought, given the risks she faced, she didn't want to visit Pan's domain. Where did she hope to go? Had she some other domain in mind, some haven she hoped to find?

Every so often, the way led into a tunnel or a cavern before emerging over the abyss once more, but we saw no domains. I was thankful; each one would be home to one of the Old Gods or some powerful demon that would threaten us.

As another gigantic slab of rock came into sight ahead, the gleaming path entering a cave at its base, I heard a distant rumble of thunder. Thorne halted and turned to face me, a look of fear in her eyes.

"What's wrong?" I asked.

Again that thunder rumbled. This time it was louder; it sounded much nearer.

"Last time I heard that sound it presaged the arrival of the demon called Tanaki. We only escaped because Alice blinded him with her magic, burning and melting his eyes."

I knew of that demon. Tanaki had fathered the wolf-like creature that had tried to slay me two years earlier; I had been on the run, carrying the Fiend's head in a sack, attempting to keep it out of the clutches of our enemies.

"Run!" cried Thorne, starting to sprint toward the entrance to the cave.

She had hardly taken two steps when, with a tremendous roar, Tanaki appeared between us and safety.

The demon was a colossus, legs straddling the path,

head fifty feet above us. It bore some resemblance to the son I had already encountered. The jaw was elongated and full of jagged wolf's teeth, but its furry body was human in shape, with huge hands that ended in murderous talons.

But one thing gave me hope: I knew that this demon had great powers of regeneration, but Alice's magic must have been extremely powerful.

I saw that its eye sockets were empty. It was still blind.

Suddenly, to my dismay, Bony Lizzie ran forward, crying out in a loud, shrill voice, "Here they are, right behind me! Here are your enemies. Their ally, the assassin Grimalkin, slayed your son. The girl, Thorne, was the accomplice of the witch who blinded you! I brought them to you as you asked. Here they are. Take them and give me my reward!"

So it was as I had expected: Lizzie had planned to betray us all along.

Without any need for communication, Thorne and I stepped ahead of Lizzie and, ignoring her, ran past the demon as it reached down toward the path with a monstrous taloned hand. That grasping hand passed just over our heads. I had killed Tanaki's son, the kretch, and then Thorne had slayed the creature a second time, here in the dark, consigning it to oblivion. Now Tanaki sought revenge, but he was blind and, guided by the information Lizzie had given him, the huge hand swept on toward the witch.

She screamed as the blind demon grasped her and brought her close to his face. I looked up and saw her jaw working as she opened her mouth to tell Tanaki of his mistake.

But she uttered no words: perhaps she was being crushed, the air driven from her lungs. Whatever the reason, the moment passed, and now Lizzie would never speak again.

The demon bit off her head, swallowed it, then threw her body into the abyss. Now she was twice dead, and consigned to oblivion.

We ran through the splayed legs of the sated Tanaki and reached the safety of the cave. Glancing back, I saw that it was still feeling around the path with its fingers, searching for another victim.

We went on through the cave, hoping to reach Pan's domain before the demon discovered our whereabouts.

7
The Domain of Pan

We followed the white path until a small green disk no larger than a star appeared in the distance. It grew and grew—until I saw that there was an immense oasis of trees and grass floating in the darkness before us. This was surely Pan's domain, I thought.

I felt a shiver as we stepped off the path and began walking through the trees. Pan was our ally in the fight against the Kobalos and their god, Talkus, but we were interlopers here, and he would not appreciate this intrusion.

The sky was dark and there was no moon, but the green light was everywhere. It radiated from the ground, the grass, the ferns, and the trees. Green was Pan's color, the color of life itself.

I hoped that it would be his benign boy form that we encountered; he'd be playing on his pipes, and we'd be able to talk to him. His other shape was so terrible that we might find ourselves driven mad or consumed by the flames of his wrath.

"This will be very dangerous," Thorne said, echoing my own thoughts. "Pan may exact a terrible price. What was the price he asked of Alice? Was it as bad as she expected? She was very afraid."

"It was even worse than she feared," I replied. "Pan demanded that she work with the dark mage Lukrasta, and join her power with his to fight the Kobalos. It meant that she had to leave Tom Ward. She obeyed Pan without explaining her actions to anyone, and a rift grew between her and Tom. She did not tell him the true reason for what had occurred until much later. But Lukrasta is dead now, slain by the Kobalos mages, and she and Tom are reconciled."

"Then what will he demand of us for entering his domain uninvited?" I was indeed concerned as to what the cost might be.

Thorne turned and tried to reassure me. "He is our ally and should welcome our offer of help. Though it's true that gods are notoriously willful and unpredictable. . . ."

I frowned. I knew that we were in great danger because of our presumption.

As my eyes adjusted to the green light, I began to

notice things. The leaves on the trees were curled and brown, as if autumn was approaching; some had already fallen onto the grass. Alice had once told me how verdant and luxurious Pan's domain was, but underfoot everything was parched and wilting. Was this the result of Pan's clash with Golgoth, the Lord of Winter? Was he really so badly wounded, his power so diminished?

Then, in the distance, I suddenly heard the sound of pipes. It was indeed the music of Pan, in his friendlier form. I pointed toward the sound and led the way, with Thorne at my heels. I remembered hearing that music once before, far away in the distance; it had been enthralling, resonating with energy and power. Now it sounded weaker, even melancholy.

Finally I caught sight of the god. He was still dressed in leaves and bark, and sat on a log playing his reed pipes—a pale boy with long, curled green toenails, unkempt fair hair, and pointy ears. However, his face was gaunt, and there were dark circles around his eyes. The hand holding the pipes seemed to tremble.

Alice had told me that when Pan played, birds flocked around his head or perched on his shoulder, while animals gamboled at his feet or stared up at him, enchanted by his music. But the only other creature present was a large black raven, perched on a branch directly above his head. The god looked like a shadow of his former self. No doubt this was a result of his clash with Golgoth.

I'd expected him to scowl at us, angered by our presence, ready to shift into his other, more terrible aspect, but he merely nodded and lowered his pipes.

"I've been expecting you." There was a note of sadness in his voice.

"You knew we were coming?" I asked, studying him.

"There is little in the dark that escapes my attention. I sensed your approach, but I do not know what you wish of me," he said with a shake of his head.

"First, I must ask your forgiveness for this intrusion," I said politely. "If there is a price to be paid for that, I am happy to pay it."

"We will speak of that later, but for now simply tell me what you want."

"We have enemies in common," I told him. "On Earth I fought against them to the best of my ability, but now I am in a place where I can do nothing further."

"That is because you are dead, Grimalkin. It is the fate of all mortals," Pan said with a weary smile.

"I have been informed that it is possible for a dead witch to return to Earth; it requires the cooperation of two gods to achieve it. Is this true?"

"Is that what you wish for?" Pan asked.

"Yes. I wish it for us both. Thorne and I wish to go back. On Earth, we could achieve much that would serve you as well."

"Well, such a contribution would indeed be useful for the fight ahead," Pan admitted. "My strength is returning only very slowly; all too soon I may have to face my enemies again. What you wish for is possible . . . though very difficult. And yes, I would need the help of another god. It will not be easy to find one willing to join with me. It could take time. Even if I do find a partner among those opposed to Talkus and Golgoth, there may be difficulties. I would have to make some sort of compromise. It might affect you directly and be unacceptable. Believe me, there are worse things than being dead and trapped in the dark."

"I can only judge that when I learn what the price is," I told him. "I thank you for listening and agreeing. Now I would like to ask you about something that puzzles me. Many of the dead here have marks or wounds that show how they died. I was slain by Golgoth, frozen solid and shattered into bloody splinters! Why am I then still whole?"

"The dark has its own rules," Pan said. "Most souls take the shape that reflects the manner of their death. However, you are exceptionally strong, Grimalkin, and thus immune to the rule that applies to other denizens of the dark. Some, such as the girl beside you, arrive damaged but are then made whole again, as a reward for some task carried out here."

He gave the faintest of smiles and came to his feet with difficulty, moving more like an old man with stiff joints and weak muscles than a boy.

"You may wait here within my domain until things are resolved," he said, turning. "I have prepared a place for you. Follow me."

As Pan set off through the trees, the raven gave a raucous cry and flew off in the opposite direction. We followed the god. His pace was slow and he walked with a limp, but we did not have to go far. I'd expected the "place" to be some sort of building; perhaps a tower or some other type of fortification.

I should have guessed its nature.

Ahead of us stood a tree of immense girth and height, set in a large clearing, its extensive boughs taking up every inch of the space available. It was deciduous, but its leaves contrasted with those I had seen so far; they were green and luxuriant, as if in the fresh new growth of spring. The tree was a gigantic, ancient oak, its trunk gnarled, the bark bulging with protuberances, but I saw that there was an opening in it, and steps leading upward.

Pan gestured toward the entrance. "One hundred steps will bring you to your quarters," he told us. "All you need will be there. But I give you warning: to me, *all* life is precious. Nothing will harm you, so tolerate its presence, wherever it is encountered."

"I will slay nothing that does not seek to harm me," I agreed.

"That is all I ask," Pan replied. "That you should be tolerant."

With that he turned and walked away into the trees. We both stared after him until he was lost from sight. I went through the doorway and began to climb the wooden steps that had been cut into the tree trunk. The hundredth step brought me to another doorway, and I stepped inside, Thorne close behind me.

There were no windows or openings to allow us to see out, but the oval room was filled with a subdued green light that radiated from the walls. It contained only one item of furniture: a round table bearing a jug and two glasses filled almost to the brim with a dark red liquid. The metallic odor told me instantly that it was blood.

To serve as beds, there were two heaps of straw. We would be comfortable enough—I had experienced far harsher conditions on my journeys through the County and elsewhere. At least we would be warm and dry here.

Then I noticed something that gave me cause for concern. Close to the ceiling was a huge spider's web; the creature that had spun it was larger than my fist and throbbed threateningly at the center. Beetles scuttled across the ceiling, and columns of ants wended their way over the floor. All these were Pan's creatures.

"Be careful where you step, child," I warned Thorne.

I wondered if Pan would be angered by the accidental death of one of these small creatures. What a human might consider of little consequence, he might view very differently. We needed to be careful. The gods were unpredictable, a law unto themselves.

Thorne nodded in agreement and stepped carefully toward the table, where she lifted one of the glasses to her lips and drank deeply from it. Then she licked her lips and looked at me. "You should try it, Grimalkin. It's cool and delicious. Surely you must hunger?"

I *was* hungry and thirsty, but not sufficiently so to drink the blood Thorne found so palatable. Even in my earliest days of training in dark magic, I had never been tempted to become a blood witch. "Perhaps I will do so after a sleep," I said.

"It's not just pangs of hunger that should concern you," Thorne insisted, pressing home her advice. "You will weaken if you don't drink some. You'll need all your strength in this dangerous place."

"If by 'this dangerous place' you mean the dark in general, then I must agree. But Pan said that nothing would harm us. Surely here, at the heart of the domain of our ally, we are safe?"

Thorne shrugged, but she didn't look happy. I lay down on the straw and was about to close my eyes when she spoke again.

"Something else I should warn you of, Grimalkin. . . . Most of those who dwell in the dark find it impossible to sleep; those who do often have terrible nightmares."

"Are you able to sleep, child?" I asked her.

"A little," she answered, "but my sleep is shallow, and dark shadows haunt my dreams. And sometimes I feel cold fingers brushing against my brow—though when I open my eyes, there's nothing there."

"I will see how I do. I am certainly weary enough to sleep."

I settled down and allowed my breathing to slow. I was aware of insects crawling over my body, but I stilled my mind. They would not hurt me. I could tolerate the itch.

Eventually I drifted off to sleep and was not troubled by dreams that I could later remember.

Suddenly, I don't know how much later, I was awakened by Thorne, who was shaking me violently by the shoulder.

"There's something trying to get in!" she cried. "Something huge!"

I could hear scratching on the wall outside our room. I had no idea how close we were to the outer trunk of the huge tree, but it sounded as if huge claws were raking against the bark. Then there was a deeper grinding sound that made the whole room vibrate, as if some powerful entity was boring through the wood, trying to get in.

I came to my feet and drew two of my long blades. Now the whole tree was shaking and swaying.

And then, as suddenly as it had started, whatever it was had gone and the sounds ceased. The green light intensified, and Pan materialized in the room.

"You needn't fear," he said. "There has been an attack upon my domain, but it has been repulsed."

"An attack—by whom?" I said as I sheathed my blades.

"It was one of the lesser gods that have allied themselves with Talkus," Pan told me.

"I thought that gods rarely fought one another directly—and certainly never intruded into each other's domains," I said.

Pan smiled grimly. "These are strange times. The usual rules have been suspended. God strives against god, and not all will survive."

Had it come to this—open war among the gods? I wondered fearfully.

"Let us speak of other things," Pan insisted. "I have found a god who might be prepared to work with me to send you back to Earth. However, she will set certain conditions that you may find unacceptable. She will tell you about them herself."

"So the god is female. What is her name?"

"It is Hecate."

I sucked in my breath angrily.

Hecate was my enemy.

8
The Journey to the Mill

Two days later, Jenny, Arkwright, and I set off for the water mill to see Judd Brinscall.

It was a bright morning, and the air was crisp and dry. The most direct route north was across the fells, but because of the ice and snow on the summits we kept to the lower slopes. That would make the journey slightly longer, but there was no need for haste.

I was carrying my staff and bag and wearing the Starblade in its shoulder scabbard. Jenny carried her own staff and bag. Arkwright had his huge staff across his shoulder and swung his own bulky bag as if untroubled by the weight.

It felt good to be alive. There were curlews swooping over the grassy slopes, and far to the west, the sea sparkled in the sunlight. I could see rabbits bobbing along in the distance, so we certainly wouldn't go hungry. The only thing that spoiled my mood was my worry that I might not get back to Chipenden before Alice returned. I'd left her a note saying we'd only be a few days, but this journey meant that we might be apart for longer than I'd hoped.

As we descended the slopes to the northeast, the sun was already going down and the sky over Morecambe Bay to the west was red, promising another fine day tomorrow. Jenny was almost as good as Alice at hunting rabbits, so by the time Bill Arkwright and I had made camp and gotten a fire going, she'd already caught and skinned three beauties.

Arkwright insisted on doing the cooking while Jenny and I watched, our mouths watering as the juices from the meat dribbled and hissed in the flames.

"Well, Master Ward, what do you reckon the next threat's likely to be?" he asked as we started to eat.

I'd already given him an account of how we'd dealt with Golgoth and the price we'd paid in doing so—the life of Grimalkin, the witch assassin, and of Meg, the lamia witch who'd once lived with John Gregory in the winter house up on Anglezarke Moor.

"Well, it isn't the end of Golgoth, that's for sure. But the winter seems to be coming to an end, so I suppose he's back in the dark licking his wounds," I finished.

"The next threat is likely to come from Talkus, or maybe Balkai, the first ranked of all the Kobalos high mages."

"Tell me more about this new god of theirs," said Arkwright.

"Well, he's supposed to take the form of a skelt."

"They're rare creatures. Do you remember the one you had that little problem with?" he asked me.

I remembered it well! The skelt had been imprisoned in a water pit under the mill but had escaped. It had scuttled toward me, hurling me to the ground and spearing my throat with its sharp bone tube. It had been draining my blood when Arkwright had attacked it with a rock.

I smiled. "You saved my life. You cracked its head open like an egg. But they're not so rare anymore. After the battle on the Wardstone, hundreds of them appeared and ripped the body of the Fiend to pieces."

"And we saw some in the far north in Kobalos territory—they can even survive in boiling water," Jenny said, joining the conversation for the first time. "We talked to a dead Kobalos mage too. He called himself the Architect, and it was through his magic that Talkus was born. His intentions were good: he hoped that Talkus would cause Kobalos females to be born again. But the Architect was slain, and others took over and changed the god's nature before his birth, making him warlike."

Arkwright was staring at Jenny, his expression easy to read: he wasn't happy for a girl to butt into a conversation between two spooks. But Jenny had been right to supply that information and share the knowledge with him. It was important that he know everything about the Kobalos. They posed a threat to the whole world. They had killed all their females, and now the only way they could reproduce was with captured human females—slaves they called purrai.

"I think it's likely that the next strike into the County will come from their new god, but he may not be alone," I said. "The Kobalos mages are able to transport themselves here. We need a magical alliance with the witch clans if we are to stand any chance against what's coming. That's why Alice has gone to Pendle. She serves Pan; together, they're a force to be reckoned with, but he's still weak after his battle with Golgoth."

"I wish we didn't need witches as allies," Jenny said. "It just seems wrong."

Arkwright shrugged. "I once thought the same myself, girl. But we have to survive somehow. Even John Gregory must have come round to that way of thinking. After all, he clearly accepted the alliance with Grimalkin."

I nodded. "Yes, he compromised in the end, as I did. It was necessary in order to survive."

* * *

The next day we set off soon after dawn, heading north toward Kendal. As usual, we skirted Caster to the east. The Quisitor, a priest who specialized in hunting witches, was now based in Priestown, but he sometimes visited Caster. He had no love for spooks; in his eyes we were no better than those who dwelled in the dark. As far as he was concerned, fighting the dark was the province of the church, and we were merely dangerous interlopers. If caught, we were just as likely to end up in the castle dungeons as any witches, so it was best to give Caster a wide berth.

Here, I remembered, they hanged witches rather than burning them. Afterward, the families collected the bodies and buried them in shallow graves in Witch Dell, just east of Pendle. The first time the full moon shone, these witches became aware and began to move. Weak ones were only able to catch mice and root around for worms, but strong ones could run faster than a man and had a thirst for blood. This made them more dangerous dead than alive. My master had once told me that the hanging of witches in Caster probably accounted for three quarters of the dead inhabitants of that dangerous dell.

Once beyond Caster, we reached the canal, crossing the first bridge we came to and heading north along its western bank. We strolled along the cinder towpath, taking our time. It was chilly, but once more the sun was shining, and it lifted my spirits. I felt optimistic and cheerful. Somehow I felt sure that somehow we'd find a way to defeat the Kobalos.

Ahead of us, long narrow barges drawn by horses were moving along the canal in both directions. There were coal barges coated in soot and grime, others were brightly painted—the routine activity belied the threat gathering on the far shore of the northern sea and the danger that might appear out of thin air. The attacks by Kobalos mages and support troops had so far taken place closer to Chipenden. As far as I knew, there had been no enemy activity in this area, which might account for the lack of concern. No doubt Judd Brinscall would be able to give us news of any local incursions.

We halted briefly for a lunch of cold rabbit and crumbly County cheese. By the time we approached the place where we had to leave the towpath, it was already dusk. It was easy enough to see the spot, despite the failing light, as it was marked by a huge post on the canal bank; it looked something like a gibbet, but instead of an executed felon, below it hung a huge bronze bell. The bargemen would ring that bell when they made deliveries to the mill.

We followed the path down the slope into the gloom.

Bill Arkwright was in the lead, Jenny bringing up the rear. To my right I could hear the gurgling of a stream, which grew louder as we approached the water mill between the drooping willows.

We reached the perimeter of the garden, a high, rusty iron fence enclosing a tangle of saplings and shrubs. Arkwright led the way left, following the curve of the railings across the soggy ground until we reached the narrow gap, which was the only entrance. Once through that, we came to the shallow moat. I was surprised when he went straight across without dipping his forefinger in the water and touching it to his lips.

Salt was regularly tipped into the moat so that water witches could not intrude. When I'd stayed at the mill, Arkwright had checked the salinity each time he returned to the house. Maybe he thought that was Judd's responsibility until he took over again.

Picking up the course of the stream again, he headed toward the huge, dilapidated mill. It still looked ready to tumble over in the next storm. Parts of it were rotting, desperately in need of repair. I'd been wondering how the dogs would greet their old master, but I heard no barks, so it seemed likely that Judd was away on spook's business. The mill was dark, and banging on the door elicited no response.

"Looks like we'll have to spend the night outdoors again . . . just when I was looking forward to a warm bed," Jenny said.

I smiled to myself. I knew that wouldn't be necessary; in my bag was the special key made by John Gregory's locksmith brother, Andrew. It would open most locks, and this one would be no problem.

But then Arkwright reached into his pocket and frowned as his hand emerged empty. "I could have sworn that I still had my key. I mean, you don't lose the key to your own home, do you, Master Ward?"

I opened my bag, shrugging. "A lot's happened since you left. It's no wonder you no longer have it. Don't worry—here's a key that'll fit the door."

He smiled and accepted it, but instead of inserting it into the lock, he led the way toward the huge water wheel without a word of explanation. Although the stream swept toward it with plenty of force, the wheel itself was immobile.

Bill Arkwright stared up at it and gave a deep sigh. "This is where my mother died," he said. "She threw herself under the wheel after my father was killed. I've been trying for days, but I just can't remember the faces of my mam and dad. That bothers me. Why can't I see them?" He gave a sob, and tears trickled down his cheeks.

I'd seen him angry, but never sad like this.

"Memories fade with time," I told him. "It happens to everyone."

"Maybe it's the drink," he suggested. "They say that too much red wine can damage your memory. There are other things I can't seem to recall. . . ."

He was probably correct, but I made no reply. Jenny caught my eye, and I could see tears brimming in her eyes too. Her empathy was allowing her to share Arkwright's feelings.

He turned and led the way back to the front door. He inserted my key, opened the door, and walked into the darkness. I carried a lantern in my bag and had intended to light it before going in, but I followed at his heels.

It was only as I stepped into the room that I felt the warning chill.

Something from the dark was lying in wait for us.

9

Dead Bodies

Despite the gloom, I recognized the danger. It was a huge skelt, one of the biggest I'd ever seen. Arkwright raised his new staff, but before he could wield it, the creature scuttled straight past him and attacked me, its deadly bone tube aimed at my throat.

I had a moment of terror. Was this more than a skelt? I wondered. Was I being attacked by Talkus?

Then my training took over, and I reacted just in time to meet its deadly charge. Holding my staff with both hands, I pressed the lever to release the blade, stabbing it down toward the skelt. However, the creature twisted away and I missed it.

It lunged forward again from my left, and I barely recovered my balance in time—but on this occasion I managed to drive the silver-alloy blade into the body, just behind the head.

The skelt writhed and struggled to break free, but then, all at once, Jenny was at my side; she stabbed the creature again and again with her own staff until it quivered and lay still.

I glanced across at Bill Arkwright, surprised that he hadn't come to my aid. Was I imagining it, or did he have a faint smile on his face?

"Well done, Master Ward! John Gregory and I taught you well. You certainly made short shrift of this skelt—you didn't need my help, did you? And you too, Mistress Jenny. That was excellent staff work. No boy apprentice could have done better!"

At that, Jenny's face lit up with a grin. I was surprised to see how well the two of them were getting along. Bill Arkwright seemed to have mellowed.

After that, we lit the lantern and I looked about me. Arkwright had never lived in this room, which was still full of empty crates. Judd had made no effort to tidy up and make it habitable, but he had removed all the empty wine bottles. I glanced toward the trapdoor in the corner. Beyond it, steps led down to the area under the mill where water witches were bound in pits.

Staying together in case of danger, we checked the house for other threats, room by room. Jenny and I entered each one cautiously, while Arkwright stayed back, seemingly content to let me lead the way.

It was as we went into the small bedroom that we had a scare that made my heart pound. Something exploded toward me out of the darkness and brushed against my hair. I stepped back, but my heart began to slow as Jenny lifted the lantern high and I saw that the room was full of swooping bats. There was a small hole high up in the wall where they'd gained access.

"Brinscall's let this place go to rack and ruin," Arkwright complained.

I thought his comment slightly unfair. This was the bedroom I'd stayed in for my training. Judd probably didn't use it and had no reason to check it.

Our search revealed nothing further, and I helped Arkwright drag the dead skelt outside. When daylight returned, we'd dump it in the marsh, but for now we left it in the yard.

"How did it manage to get across the salt moat?" he mused as we headed back into the kitchen. "I wonder if Brinscall has been slacking. Complacency can be a very dangerous thing in our line of work."

"I don't think Judd is likely to be guilty of that," I said in his defense. "Maybe he's been away for some time and the saltwater's become diluted?"

"Well, I'll check the moat tomorrow. Better to be safe than sorry."

By now Jenny had lit the large stove in the kitchen, and the room was starting to warm up. Opening the door to the larder, I found a moldy loaf of bread, some salted beef, a bundle of carrots, turnips, and rutabagas, and a few bunches of dried herbs hanging from hooks. Arkwright set to work cooking a stew. It was delicious, and soon after we'd eaten we settled down on our blankets on the floor. The rest of the house was too damp to be comfortable.

At first light I accompanied Arkwright to the moat. He dipped his finger into the water, touched it to his tongue, then spat it out with a frown.

"As I thought, there's hardly any salt in it at all!" he exclaimed.

We found bags of salt in the storeroom, so I helped him to carry them over and pour the contents into the moat at intervals. That done, we tipped the dead skelt into a particularly soggy part of the marsh, washed our hands, and went in to breakfast—the last of last night's stew warmed up.

"Perhaps we should show your apprentice the pits?" Arkwright suggested.

"Good idea," I said. Jenny had visited the mill when I came to talk to Judd, but she'd never seen the pits.

I turned to her. "The pits are full of water because marsh- and water-based denizens of the dark abound here, Jenny. There might even be a water witch. It would be useful for you to see one. Then you'd understand the nature of the threat they pose."

Arkwright grasped the iron ring and lifted the trapdoor. Holding the lantern, he led the way down the wooden steps into the dark area below the mill. I could hear the sound of the stream rushing over the pebbles toward the huge immobile wheel. Although he'd never confirmed it, I guessed that the wheel had not turned since the day it had crushed and drowned his poor mother.

I reached the bottom and stepped down onto the mud. This was no flagged cellar; it was just a flat, muddy area with the wheel and stream on one side. The stone foundations of the mill, topped by wood, formed the three other walls.

It stank of rotten wood, damp . . . and something else; something rank and sweet.

I had smelled it before, more than once. Something had died down here. It was the odor of rotting flesh.

Arkwright lifted the lantern high above his head, and I glanced about. It looked as if the bars to the pits had been torn away—and with some violence. Heavy hammers and chisels could have been responsible, but the metal frames were distorted, twisted as if a giant had attacked them in a demented rage.

We walked to the edge of the nearest pit and looked down. The water was still; nothing moved, although something could have been lurking beneath the surface. I readied my staff, releasing the blade. Both skelts and water witches could move with terrifying speed. They could drag you into the water and drain your blood so speedily that you didn't even have time to drown.

Arkwright shook his head and led the way to the next pit. We checked them, one by one. Each was the same: the metal bars had been removed, but the water was still and seemingly empty.

Then, just beyond the final pit, the one closest to the waterwheel, we found the source of that terrible stench.

Two bodies were laid out side by side. One was human; the other was a dog.

"Tell me we're not seeing this, Master Ward!" Arkwright exclaimed.

I made no reply but covered my mouth and nose with my hand. I could hear Jenny retching behind me. Both bodies were badly decomposed: bones showed through rotting flesh, so it wasn't easy to tell what had killed them. There were no obvious wounds.

I felt saddened and shocked. These had to be the remains of one of the wolfhounds and Judd Brinscall. Judd and I hadn't always seen eye to eye, but I respected the man, and he'd been a good spook. It was a loss to the County.

"Poor dog . . . but is it Blood or Bone?" Arkwright said, shaking his head. "I wonder what happened to the other one."

He seemed remarkably untouched by the dog's death, and I thought he should also have expressed some regret at the fate Judd had suffered.

"Is it Brinscall for sure?" he asked.

I stared at the body. The face was gone, but the corpse was wearing the hooded gown of a spook.

"It's Judd Brinscall, all right," said Jenny, her voice hardly more than a whisper as she came to my side. "Look. You can see the two fingers missing from his right hand."

That was conclusive. He'd had his fingers bitten off by a witch at the Battle of the Wardstone.

"What killed them, Master Ward?" Arkwright said.

"Maybe it was skelts," I answered. "With bodies so badly decomposed, you wouldn't see the puncture marks. But judging by the damage to the bars on the pits, something else accompanied them."

For how could skelts have wrenched off the metal bars? They didn't have arms or that kind of strength. Even if they had killed Judd and the dog, something else had been involved. Something else from the dark had been here.

10
What Am I?

There was no point contacting the local priest. From their past dealings, Arkwright knew that he was more hostile to spooks than most. Not only would he not allow a spook to be buried in his churchyard, he wouldn't even bless the corpse.

We buried Judd and the dog—it was impossible to know which one it was—in the garden, in the same grave; I knew that he'd grown fond of Blood and Bone.

As we filled in the soil, Jenny uttered the only prayer. "May they rest in peace," she said softly.

"Do you think dogs have souls, girl?" Arkwright asked, a touch of truculence in his voice.

Jenny nodded. "They have as much soul as we do," she replied. "You can see it in their eyes."

I thought Arkwright was going to argue, but he simply gave a sigh and walked away.

I followed him back to the house. It was already late afternoon, and the light was beginning to fail.

"Are you going to stay here?" I asked.

"It was what I intended on the journey over," he remarked, "but now I'm not so sure. I can't hunt water witches across the marsh without dogs. I'd need to get a couple of pups and train 'em up. That'll take time. Not only that. I think we should stick together. There's safety in numbers. What killed Brinscall might come back. I think I'll base myself at Chipenden with you—that's if you don't mind, Master Ward?"

I nodded and smiled. "That's what I was hoping you'd say. We face a terrible threat, and we need to combine our strength. Shall we spend the night here and then set off tomorrow morning?"

So it was agreed. All we had left to eat were vegetables, but Arkwright produced the best broth I'd tasted in a long time.

Afterward we sat by the stove, and he started to read a book he'd brought down from the bedroom where he'd once kept his parents' coffins. Some of the books had already been taken to Chipenden to stock John Gregory's library after the old one had been destroyed by fire. We decided to carry a few more back to Chipenden—the damp in this empty house would do them no good at all.

I looked at Jenny. She was sitting quietly, staring into space. She hadn't said very much since we'd found the bodies. She looked sad.

I watched Arkwright as he read, his brow furrowed in concentration. The light from the candles wasn't strong, and he was holding it quite close. I noted the title on the spine: *Morwena*.

It was a book he himself had written about the fiercest water witch that had ever lived. Years earlier, I'd read parts of it myself when she'd threatened us.

Suddenly he looked up and stared at me. "Do you know, Master Ward, when I read this book, every word seems fresh and new. I wrote it, but I don't remember doing so. It could easily be the work of someone else. Isn't that strange?"

"Maybe it's something all writers feel when they read their own work years after writing it," I replied. "I sometimes feel the same when reading my early notebooks. We change, don't we? I'm very much older than the young boy who began his first notebook as a twelve-year-old apprentice."

He nodded doubtfully, then continued to read.

After another twenty minutes, he put the book down. "Shall we turn in for the night?" he said.

It was really a statement of intent rather than a

question—a polite order. The Bill Arkwright of old had been like that. He naturally assumed command. After all, we were in his house.

Jenny and I both nodded, and he blew out all the candles but the one on the stove. Jenny and I were wrapping ourselves in our blankets when he suddenly came across and knelt close to me, staring into my eyes.

"I see you're quite fond of that rusty sword, Master Ward," he said.

"Fond?" I asked, raising my eyebrows. "What do you mean?"

"Well, not only do you wear it in that shoulder scabbard all day; it shares your bed at night too. You sleep with one hand on it!"

"I do that for a reason. This sword may not be much to look at, but it was forged by Grimalkin, and she put her most powerful magic into it. It will never break and cuts clean through the strongest armor. It protects me against any dark magic that seeks to harm me. The Kobalos mages could attack at any time, so I'd be a fool to let it out of my sight."

"Do you think I could examine it for a moment, Master Ward?" he asked. "I'd like to feel what it's like to hold such a weapon." And he stretched his hand out to take the Starblade.

Warning bells were jangling in my head. Handing it over to him didn't feel right. I thought I'd accepted that this was indeed Bill Arkwright, but now I realized that something deep inside me still wasn't sure.

I was going to refuse, but before I could speak, Jenny intervened.

"Grimalkin said that Tom shouldn't allow anybody else to touch it," she lied quickly. "Contact with another would bleed away some of its power."

I tried not to betray my true feelings and simply nodded. So Jenny didn't trust him either, I realized.

"I'm sorry, but Jenny's right," I said.

Arkwright withdrew his hand, frowned, then nodded. He said nothing, and moments later he blew out the final candle. I was tired and felt myself drifting off to sleep. But I gripped the hilt of the Starblade tightly so that, even when deeply asleep, I would not release it.

After breakfast Arkwright said he was going for a walk across the marsh as far as the ruined monastery and back.

"I used to sit there sometimes and think my problems through," he told me. "I'd like to do it again this morning. I've a few things on my mind, and it might be some time before I return to the mill."

I looked out through the doorway. There was a mist thickening over the marsh, and the visibility was already down to a few feet.

"Probably be best if we all go," I suggested. "Anything could be out there in these conditions."

Water witches often gathered on the marsh under cover of darkness; this mist would also shroud their presence. Without the dogs to give warning, Arkwright would be at risk.

"I can look after myself, Master Ward, so don't you go worrying about me. I need to be alone so I can think things through."

Jenny and I stood watching as he walked off into the mist.

"So what was that all about last night, Jenny? You still don't trust him?" I asked.

"The feelings I get from him are fine. He's rough and tough, though his heart seems to be in the right place. But he's a troubled man—there's something wrong, Tom. I can't put my finger on it. Perhaps I'm just being foolish, but I sensed danger when he reached for the sword. Luckily I managed to come up with something quickly."

"You were right to trust your instincts," I told her. "And it's always better to be cautious. I'm still not sure about him myself. I wasn't going to allow him to take the blade, but you made things easy for me. Thanks for helping out."

Jenny smiled and was silent for a while. Then, suddenly, she asked me, "When I complete my apprenticeship, what will happen?"

I was surprised by her question, coming as it did when we were under threat, but I supposed she had to think of the future.

"Well, you'll be a spook and will look after your own territory, keeping it safe from the dark, as you'll have been trained to do. You could base yourself here at the mill, if you like. That way we wouldn't have far to travel if some difficulty reared its head."

Jenny shivered. "I don't like it here. This is the last place I'd want to work."

"Then what about taking the Anglezarke house?"

"I hate that cold windy moor too. I like Chipenden. Couldn't I stay there and share the workload with you?"

"Yes, you could certainly do that for a while. After completing his apprenticeship, John Gregory shared the Chipenden territory with his own master. You could do the same, but eventually you'd need to strike out on your own. It's part of the process of developing the responsibilities of a spook. Most of my master's apprentices—the ones who didn't run away or die learning the trade—went off to distant parts of the County to practice."

We lapsed into silence, then started to gather our things together for the journey, splitting the books between our bags. They would be heavy, but unlike my dead master, John Gregory, I rarely made my apprentice carry mine as well as hers.

It was then that we heard a scratching and a whining outside. It sounded like a dog, but I gripped my staff as I slowly inched the door open. A big wolfhound limped into the kitchen. It was a sorry sight, its fur wet and caked with mud, with scratches all over its body. It looked up at us pitifully.

I knelt down and started petting it while it licked my face and panted. Jenny was nervous and kept her distance. Once, when she'd persisted in asking him to train her as a spook, Judd had set the wolfhounds on her.

"So one of the dogs survived the attack," she said. "Poor thing. Which one is it—Blood or Bone?"

"I think this is Blood," I replied. They were hard to tell apart, but there was a small gray streak behind Blood's left ear.

"Wish dogs could talk," Jenny said. "Blood would be able to tell us what happened here."

"Well, we'll be taking her back to Chipenden with us.

It'll be good to have a dog around again. This should certainly cheer Bill Arkwright up!"

Our preparations for the journey completed, we waited in the front room. I sat on an empty crate, and the dog settled at my feet. Jenny began to pace, no doubt impatient to be off.

I glanced around the room, and as usual my eyes were drawn toward the trapdoor in the corner. I wondered what had released the bound water witches, what had ripped away those grilles. . . . It must have been something with incredible strength or magical power. Had Balkai been here?

Suddenly Blood began to growl, her fur standing on end. I heard approaching footsteps. Was it Arkwright? No—surely it must be danger of some kind. The wolfhound was staring at the door and trembling.

As I came to my feet, it slowly opened, creaking on its rusty hinges to reveal Bill Arkwright silhouetted against the gray morning light. He stood perfectly still as he stared at us, gripping his staff with its fearsome blade.

Blood rose to her feet and growled again before advancing toward him carefully. By rights she should have bounded up, barking joyfully, to lick him and to be petted in return. But her steady advance was as if toward a threat. She looked as if she was about to attack him!

Nor did he call out a welcome. I'd have expected him to be pleased to find that one of his dogs had survived. But he took four rapid steps into the room and raised his staff, his face twisted in fury, then brought it down hard, the blade aimed directly at the dog.

He was fast. But Jenny was faster.

She stepped forward and blocked his lethal thrust with her own staff. The dog bounded away into the corner of the room, and for a moment Jenny and Arkwright stood there, as immobile as statues, glaring at each other. Then he spun on his heel and strode out of the house without a word.

This was beyond strange.

"Stay here!" I ordered Jenny, and went after him.

I didn't turn around to check that she'd obeyed me, but I might as well have been talking to the wall. I could hear her following close behind me.

Arkwright was heading toward the waterwheel. When I caught up with him, he was staring down again at the dark turbulent water churning over the banks of stones on either side of it.

"Why would I try to kill my own dog, Master Ward?" he asked, his expression bleak as he turned to look at me.

"It was just your natural reaction to the threat. It happened so quickly. You just acted instinctively, that's all," I said, offering him an excuse.

He was clearly troubled. "I had enough time to think. I could have used the other end of my staff, and well you know it!" he retorted. "Why did I target my dog with my blade? And why did she attack me in the first place?"

"She hadn't seen you for a long time. She fought whatever killed Judd and was traumatized. She didn't know what she was doing."

The man's expression was full of torment. Why had he behaved like that? It seemed as if he wasn't in control of himself.

"No! I'm the one who doesn't know what he's doing. There are too many things wrong with me. My memory's in pieces. I can't remember things I *should* remember. And I would never try to kill my own dog, no matter what the circumstances. That leads me to just one logical conclusion. . . ."

He paused and glanced down at the wheel again. Then he opened his mouth to speak—but he never got the words out. Jenny spoke for him.

"You're not Bill Arkwright," she said.

He looked at me, then at Jenny. "You're right, little cat. I'm not Bill Arkwright. So what am I?"

"You're something from the dark!" she exclaimed.

Suddenly the puzzle inside my head was solved, like a

key finally turning in a rusty lock. This entity was indeed from the dark—but we weren't facing a Kobalos mage who'd taken on Bill Arkwright's shape. This thing had been created to really believe that it *was* Bill Arkwright.

However, it had problems with its memory. The key to what this creature was lay in its uncertainties about its own identity.

"You're a tulpa!" I exclaimed.

Grimalkin

11
Queen of the Witches

I found it hard to believe that Pan should have chosen Hecate to be his partner. I shook my head. "Hecate is not an acceptable ally," I told him. "She is an enemy of the Pendle witches, as you know only too well!"

Long ago, Hecate had taken for herself the title Queen of the Witches, and all the clans on Earth had sworn to serve her, accepting that she was second in rank only to the Fiend. Later she had taken the side of the Caledonian witches who had invaded the County and tried to take the Pendle district for themselves, coveting its potential for dark magic.

After a close-fought battle, in which there had been heavy casualties on both sides, the witches from Caledonia had been driven back north. But we Pendle witches had never forgiven Hecate for fighting with them, and we no longer accepted her as our queen.

"She may have been the enemy of your Pendle witch

clans, but the situation has changed," Pan replied. "Now she is my ally—just as you asked of me—and will fight against the Kobalos and their gods. I badly need her support, and you, Grimalkin, *must* work with her. There is no other way you can return to Earth. She is waiting for you now on the forest path."

He shimmered, and then faded from view, and I looked at Thorne and shook my head. "Hecate is mean and vindictive. I fear that her demands will be harsh," I said.

"We have little choice," Thorne replied.

"I agree. Let us go and see what she wants in return for her aid."

We descended the stairs and stepped out onto the grass. Previously there had been no path, but now I could see black pebbles meandering away from us through the forest. Overhead there was a full moon.

I led the way, my feet crunching on the pebbles, announcing our approach. I had thought we were safe here in Pan's domain, but I felt anxious. Hecate was linked to the moon, and from it she drew part of her power. The sudden appearance of such a moon suggested that she had brought its manifestation with her. After all, this domain belonged to Pan, and Alice had told me that his sky was always dark; the only source of light was that green glow.

Pan was still weak after his fight with Golgoth. Could he protect us against Hecate if she became hostile? *Would* he protect us? After all, she was a goddess, so he probably considered her the more important ally. We were no doubt expendable.

Let Hecate do her worst, I thought. We would not go down without a fight.

I would have stepped off the path to avoid making so much noise, but now the forest had closed in, and saplings and scrub came right to the edge. But soon the undergrowth receded again, and I had a clear view of what awaited us.

Directly ahead I saw a crossroads, a tall, dark, cowled figure standing at its center. Hecate. I could feel the malevolence radiating from her.

Before her stood a huge, bubbling black cauldron from which yellow steam rose. It was at least six feet in diameter and was almost as high as Hecate's shoulder. Her left hand rested casually upon its rim, her fingers stroking the metal, and she was smirking.

Cauldrons were traditionally forged from iron to contain the powerful dark magic spells brewed within them. Yet iron caused witches pain and could weaken them; they often used servants to tend and move them. By caressing the iron rim, Hecate was demonstrating her strength. But she did not impress me. I could do the same. Throughout my life as a witch assassin, I had worked to raise my tolerance of pain.

I looked up and saw, on the branches above her head, three large ravens regarding us with silent malice.

"Do those birds serve the witch?" I asked Thorne.

"Yes," she replied. "They are watchers, able to report to her on events in the world of the living. I have used such creatures myself."

"Stay slightly to my left and to my rear," I warned her. "At my signal, draw your blades."

"How can we fight a goddess?" she whispered as we approached the tall, intimidating figure.

"We may have no choice, child," I replied. "If we are to die again, then so be it. But I will not go down without a fight."

It was significant that Hecate had chosen to meet us at such a place. She was linked to crossroads, where she would snatch souls or confront her enemies. Four ways radiated from her cauldron, and she determined the right of passage and direction of those she preyed upon. She was also known as the Goddess of the Crossroads.

I halted five paces from the cauldron and smiled at her politely, though I did not bow, as she might have expected. She would be aware of the challenge.

"You know what we wish for," I told her. "We are here to learn the price that we must pay."

"Indeed, Grimalkin, there is always a price to pay for the services of a deity," said Hecate with a grim smile. "What you wish for can be achieved. I will join my power with that of Pan, and you will be returned to Earth. But it will not be as you imagine. What *do* you think it will be like?"

"As long as I can use my weapons to destroy the Kobalos and free their female slaves, nothing else matters," I replied.

"Bravely spoken, but now I will tell you exactly what you will experience. Do not think that you will go back with a beating heart and warm blood coursing through your veins. You will never again dine on fish or meat or berries. Nor will you sip cool water from mountain streams or feel the warmth of the sun on your skin. At first, each return to Earth will be extremely painful, and you may only dwell there during the hours of darkness. Before the cock crows, you must return to the dark, or else be burned to ashes by the first rays of the morning sun. Are you prepared to accept that?" she asked.

"I am," I told her. "By what means will I journey between Earth and the dark?"

"By an act of will and an acceptance of the pain of

transit. Wish it, and it will be done."

"What weapons and powers will I have in order to fight and defeat our enemies?" I wanted to know.

"You will have what you had before—your blades, scissors, and martial skills. Additionally, you will have greater speed and strength. During the hours of darkness, you will be invisible, if you so wish, able to move swiftly and silently and slay with impunity. You will be my dark assassin, and the Kobalos mages and their dark army will be your primary target."

"For what you offer, that price is acceptable," I told her.

Hecate smiled. "I fear that you misunderstand me somewhat, Grimalkin. I outlined the *conditions* of your return to Earth. I have not yet stated the *price*."

I did not like the gloating smile that illuminated the goddess's face. I feared that the price she asked would indeed be terrible.

I was correct.

"The price is the blood of the girl who cowers behind you."

Thorne stepped forward, but I put my finger to my lips to bid her to remain silent.

"Why do you need the blood of Thorne?" I demanded angrily. "Why do you demand that particular price?"

"The girl has great bravery and potential. Her blood holds power. She took the thumb bones of the demon Beelzebub and now wears them around her neck. I will drain her blood and take her bones and wear them around *my* neck, next to those of the demon. Thus my own strength will be enhanced." Hecate had a gloating expression on her face. "For what I offer, the price must be great. In taking the blood of Thorne and casting her into oblivion, I will be hurting you, Grimalkin. You failed to protect her back on Earth, and now you will fail again. That will cause you terrible grief. It will give me great satisfaction to triumph over one of the Pendle witches, the foolish clan that rebelled against my rule."

I reached down and stroked the hilt of a throwing dagger, tensing myself for action. Then I drew in a deep breath and relaxed.

"Thorne and I need to confer about this," I told the dark queen. "If we agree to your demands, we will require a little more time together to say our farewells."

"You may take a little time, but not too much. The threat from our enemies grows steadily. I will be waiting here at the crossroads to hear your decision."

I glanced up at the three ravens, then turned and led Thorne back down the black-pebble path to the tree. We climbed the steps and entered our chamber in silence. I removed my blades and scissors from their sheaths and laid them carefully down in a row.

I spat upon my whetstone, then picked up each weapon in turn and began to sharpen it carefully.

"Why are you sharpening your blades, Grimalkin?" Thorne asked.

"All the better to cut things with."

12
The Boiling Cauldron

One by one I sharpened my blades, returning each to its leather sheath—except my favorite one, which I handed to Thorne.

"Do not sheathe this," I told her. "Tuck it into the belt of your skirt and cover its hilt with your jerkin."

I picked up my snippy scissors, spat upon the whetstone again, and sharpened them with great care. Finally I retuned the scissors to the sheath under my left armpit and smiled at Thorne.

"The bones of the demon Beelzebub that you wear around your neck—would you give them to me? I would ask to borrow them, but I'll need to drain all their power, and they will be useless afterward. So it must be a gift."

"Of course you may have them, Grimalkin," Thorne said, removing her necklace of thumb bones and extracting the two largest ones.

She handed them to me. Each had a small hole drilled through it, so it was but the work of a minute to thread them onto my own necklace.

"You mean to fight her, don't you?" Thorne asked. "You needn't do that, Grimalkin. I'm not happy dwelling in the dark. At times the prospect of oblivion appears attractive. I'd be at peace, free of the terrors of this place; free of the terrible struggle to survive. I'll willingly sacrifice myself so that you can return to Earth and slay our enemies."

"No sacrifice is required, child. Raise your spirits and ignite that flame of courage that once burned so brightly. Do you remember when I asked you to attack that bear?"

Thorne nodded and smiled. We both recalled what had happened. When she was no more than ten, the girl had pestered me to train her as a witch assassin. In an effort to discourage her, I'd challenged her to attack a fierce bear with just a knife. I promised that if she succeeded, I'd train her. She had trembled with fear, her whole body shaking, and I had waited for her to run away, hoping that she would never bother me again.

But she had run in the opposite direction—straight at the bear. She was seconds from death when I threw my dagger into its eye to kill it.

"I remember eating the bear's heart," Thorne said. "It was the most delicious thing I'd ever tasted. The day we killed that bear and you took me on and began to train me was the happiest of my entire life. It still is."

"*I* killed the bear!" I laughed. "You only stabbed it in the foot and angered it. Nonetheless, it was a brave thing to do. Deciding to train you was one of the best decisions I ever made. So hold on to that memory, and gather your courage for what we must do now."

"And what is that, Grimalkin?" Thorne asked.

"We are going to do what should have been done long ago. We are going to slay Hecate."

I explained very carefully what I intended to do, and also the part that Thorne must play. Her eyes widened as I outlined my plan, and then they shone with excitement.

This was the Thorne I remembered.

We walked down the steps and out of the tree, and began to stroll along the black path toward the crossroads. Soon the tall, stern figure of Hecate came into view, standing beside her bubbling cauldron. The three ravens were still perched on the branches above her head.

We came to a halt less than five steps from where she waited.

"Well? What have you decided?" she demanded.

As arranged, Thorne stepped in front of me, and I placed a hand on each of her shoulders.

"Thorne has agreed to sacrifice herself so that I may fight our enemies on Earth once more. All I ask is that you drain her blood quickly and hurt her as little as possible."

Hecate smiled. "There will be no pain at all, Grimalkin. I will be gentle. Let the girl come to me!"

Thorne stepped forward as bidden. I had already used some of my magic to create an illusion. Hecate would see the demon's bones still attached to Thorne's necklace. She would not realize that I was wearing them until it was too late.

When Thorne reached her, the witch queen put a hand gently on her head and bent her neck so that her throat was accessible. She opened her mouth wide and smiled, anticipating the taste of the girl's blood. But as her teeth approached Thorne's neck, her expression suddenly changed to one of fury.

The illusion I had created could not stand such close scrutiny from one so powerful.

She snarled with rage.

But it was already too late.

Thorne had plunged my favorite dagger into Hecate's heart. She twisted it three times, as I'd instructed. By then I was at her side; I seized Hecate by her long hair and bashed her head as hard as I could against the edge of the iron cauldron. I had hoped that it might crack like an egg, but to my disappointment it remained intact, and I feared that the struggle would be difficult and prolonged.

And so it proved. It would not be easy to slay the Queen of the Witches.

She fought back with terrible strength, placing her hands around my throat and choking me. But I am Grimalkin and am not so easily defeated.

Thorne was still piercing Hecate's body again and again, and that distracted the goddess sufficiently for me to change my grip from her hair to her shoulder. With a tremendous heave I thrust her head down into the cauldron so that it was submerged beneath the surface of the boiling liquid. For a few moments I managed to keep her under—but still she fought back and threw me off before hurling Thorne to her knees.

Now Hecate was a terrible sight to behold. I did not know the ingredients of the bubbling concoction, but its effects on her were terrible to behold. Apart from her eyes, every bit of flesh and hair had been removed from her head. Now there was a white skull atop a neck still retaining its flesh and sinew. But those fierce eyes still glared from their sockets, and I felt the goddess gathering her powers and preparing to blast us into nothingness. I tried to draw my blades and attack, but it was as if an invisible wall lay between us. Hecate had summoned a magical barrier. I could not take a single step toward her.

I had just one chance to turn defeat into victory. I reached for the necklace around my neck, and with my left hand I stroked the bones of Beelzebub.

The demon's strength flowed into me, and suddenly I felt strong again. I surged forward, breaking through Hecate's barrier. Then I thrust her skull back deep into the cauldron and bit her shoulder, just below the neck, sinking my teeth into her flesh, my face only inches from the boiling liquid.

I sucked her blood into my mouth. It was surprisingly sweet and tasted more like honey than blood. Still she fought, but the more she struggled, the faster I drank, gulping down her blood—until at last I felt her begin to weaken.

As I drank, I felt transformed. I was still Grimalkin, but I was also something much more.

I drank and drank until no more blood was to be had. As I drained the final drops, I felt Hecate's body shudder; above my head I heard the beating of wings as the three ravens took flight. I lifted the Queen of the Witches and pushed her down into the boiling cauldron.

Standing well back, Thorne and I watched as the huge iron vessel hissed and churned, spurting liquid into the air. But finally the fierce bubbling became a mild simmer; eventually the surface calmed, reflecting the moon like a mirror.

Moments later, stripped of every piece of skin, flesh, sinew, and clothing, the skeleton of Hecate floated to the surface. Thorne and I had triumphed, but now we'd need another god to partner Pan and aid our return to Earth. Swiftly, wasting no time, I used my scissors and snipped away Hecate's thumb bones.

I held them out to Thorne. "Take these in exchange for what you so freely gave," I invited her.

"No, Grimalkin. They are yours. You slayed Hecate, not I," she said, shaking her head.

"I slayed the bear!" I laughed. "But *we* slayed Hecate. Without your help I could not have prevailed. Take them—I insist. I have the blood of Hecate within me, and I now own her power!"

Thorne accepted the bones, and we sat on the grass at the edge of the crossroads while she carefully drilled each of Hecate's thumb bones before threading them onto her necklace.

We walked back down the path toward a second confrontation. Pan was sitting on one of the huge gnarled roots that radiated from the great tree. He was alone. No animals sat at his feet; no birds perched upon his sagging shoulders. Apart from his clothes of brown bark and green grass, his pointy ears and curly toenails, he might have been any unhappy young boy.

As we approached, he looked up and shook his head. "Why did you do it, Grimalkin?" he asked wearily.

"First, because I am the assassin of the Malkin clan, and although I am dead, I still consider it my duty to seek out and slay our enemies. Second, in exchange for her help, she demanded the blood of Thorne, which I considered vindictive, vengeful, and unreasonable. So I took her blood instead. Thus we have slain Hecate."

"You certainly *are* dead, Grimalkin, and the Malkins will find another assassin to replace you. You should not have slain our ally. You wished to fight our enemies back on Earth, but who will now join with me to send you there? I asked other gods, but they refused."

"I am still Grimalkin," I told Pan. "But I am now much more. Hecate visited the Earth at will. Perhaps I can do the same."

But as I spoke, Pan vanished without replying.

"We have become the slayers of gods!" Thorne exclaimed enthusiastically, beaming at me.

"Perhaps that's what we were always meant to be, Thorne," I told her.

"Who shall we slay next?" she demanded.

Talkus was the obvious choice, but first we had to find him.

13
Females Are Animals

We turned and walked back down the path toward the crossroads. I peered into the cauldron. The surface was still calm. Of the bones of Hecate there was now no sign. Perhaps they had dissolved.

I felt strong and confident, and filled with an energy far greater than I had ever enjoyed back on Earth. I placed my hands upon the rim of the cauldron and felt the burning pain that iron inflicts upon witches. I ignored it and concentrated, sensing the vast power within. I began to draw upon it, adding to the strength I had drained from Hecate.

I glanced down the path that I was facing. Hecate's death meant that she could no longer work with Pan to return me to Earth . . . but she had controlled the destiny of others, sending their lives down different paths. Could I use the paths to carry me back to Earth unaided? After all, Hecate had visited Earth to receive the obeisance of her subjects at the four main witches' sabbaths.

If *she* could do it, then why shouldn't I do the same? I had taken her blood into my dead body, and I possessed her magical cauldron. Did I even need the help of Pan? I wondered.

I turned to Thorne. "I'm going to attempt to return to Earth," I told her.

"Take me with you, Grimalkin," she demanded.

"Later, Thorne," I said, my hand on her shoulder. "Let me check that it is possible first."

I concentrated, drawing more power from the cauldron. The pathway ahead of me began to shimmer, then moved widdershins, against the clock. The four paths were now spinning like a wheel, with the cauldron at its hub. It was hard not to grow dizzy, and I heard Thorne gasp at the spectacle. But the area around the cauldron was stationary. As long as we didn't move, we were safe.

Suddenly I saw that there were more than four paths. As I watched, they multiplied, each of the four replicating madly. Faster and faster they spun; at the end of each I could see different scenes: villages, cathedral spires, seascapes, and farms. Each path led somewhere—there seemed to be an infinite number of destinations.

Where did I want to go on my first journey back to the land of the living?

Valkarky! Why not? I would spy upon the city of my enemies.

No sooner had I made that decision than the multitude of paths began to spin more slowly; there were now fewer of them. When the vortex came to a halt, I could see only the original four. I gazed down the narrow path ahead of me; in the distance, beyond a line of trees, I saw the city of Valkarky gleaming as white as snow—beneath a dark sky. This was important: I knew that I could not visit Earth during the hours of daylight. I knew that it was after midnight there; seven more hours remained before the dawn.

"That is where I am going!" I said, pointing toward the city. "This will be my first journey back to Earth."

"Please take me with you, Grimalkin!" Thorne begged again. "I am willing to accept the risk."

"I will do so when I've completed this visit," I told her. "Be patient, child. Besides, you have an important task to perform. Stand here and guard the cauldron so that I may return safely. Warn off any who dare approach, but if the threat is too great, call out my name. I will hear that warning and speed back to your side."

Thorne nodded, then lowered her eyes in disappointment. I smiled at her, knowing that I needed to test my abilities and determine the limits of what I could now do.

I considered my options. I could strike at the triumvirate—the three highest Kobalos mages, who ruled the others. But perhaps it would be wise to start with something easier. Perhaps I should just enter Valkarky and see if I could wander around undetected.

It would be foolish to let hubris, the sin of overweening pride, be my undoing. Lukrasta had been the most powerful of human mages, and Alice's magical power was probably greater than that of any other witch. Yet they had both underestimated the Kobalos high mages, and had been lucky to survive. I would not make the same mistake.

I began to follow the path, concentrating hard, attempting to choose the spot where I would come down—within the shadow of the city wall.

As I reached the end, I suddenly felt myself falling. As Hecate had warned me, the pain of transit from the dark to Earth was indeed terrible. As I plummeted like a stone, my blood seemed to boil, burning me from within, while my skin was seared as if by frost. My bones warped and twisted, my sinews stretching as if my whole body was on a torture rack that sought to dislocate my bones.

While alive, the most terrible pain I had ever suffered was when the silver pin was inserted to mend my shattered leg. This was far worse.

I hit the ground hard, then crouched and vomited onto the cold earth. Slowly the pain subsided, but it was many minutes before I was able to stand, and my legs shook. I realized that this was when I would always be at my most vulnerable—I had been wise to choose the cloaking shadows of the castle wall.

I looked about me. Where was the path that led back to the dark? Without it I could not return before the sun rose. I looked up and saw it shimmering in the air, a faint tube of purple light about fifty feet above my head. Reaching it would be a problem, I realized.

Then I became aware of something strange. I was no longer breathing; nor did I feel any need to take a breath. My body was strangely still. I placed my hand against my chest. My heart was not beating.

It was just as Hecate had warned. Still, what did it matter?

I could move.

I could think.

I could slay my enemies.

I was still Grimalkin.

I had come to Earth in the far north, deep within the Arctic Circle, by the very walls of the Kobalos city, Valkarky. But there were no guards around, no patrols; nothing that presented any danger to me.

I had deliberately chosen a section of wall that was still under construction. High above me, outlined against a bright swathe of stars, the sixteen-limbed creatures known collectively as the whoskor writhed and twitched as they worked to extend the city. They used skoya, a soft stone, as building material; they exuded it from their mouths and worked it with dexterous limbs.

The Kobalos believed that their city would never stop growing, that it would extend beyond their domain of ice and snow to cover the whole Earth. Not a single blade of grass would remain.

No wonder Pan was the enemy of the Kobalos and their gods. He was the deity of nature and life; he could not allow the world to be reduced to this.

I looked up and saw the whoskor working diligently above me, so absorbed in their never-ending task that there was little likelihood of their noticing me.

It was time to test my abilities.

I had traveled much during my life on Earth and studied many different types of magic. A Romanian witch had taught me elements of shamanism, but I had only developed my skill fully in one aspect: I had learned to project my soul from my body. But would it still work now that I was no longer alive?

Using my will and uttering the words of the spell in

the correct cadence, I attempted to cast my soul forward from my body. I soon became a small glowing orb of silver light. But when I glanced down, to my surprise, there was no sign of the body that my soul had temporarily abandoned.

Where had it gone? If it had vanished, how could I return to it? But once more I exerted my will and found myself standing, in human form, below the high walls of the city.

Now I understood. I was dead and part of the dark. My powers were different now. I could do more than just project my soul, leaving my body vulnerable to enemies who might stumble across it. I could now shift my shape immediately into that of an orb.

So that was one problem solved. When it was time to return to the dark, I could simply soar back up to the pathway.

There was another skill I wanted to test. When I'd lived on Earth, the ground that I walked upon and the walls that enclosed me had been solid. What would happen now? Would it be the same here?

I willed myself back into the form of an orb and floated toward the city wall, then passed right through it. The stone was very thick, and for moments I could see nothing, but then I found myself in a long, straight corridor.

I drifted to the end and entered a large chamber.

Immediately I realized that I was in one of the skleech pens where the Kobalos kept their purrai. It was full of enslaved human females. They were dressed in rags, and their faces and arms were filthy. Most were chained to the wall, some in what must have been very uncomfortable positions. Their eyes were mostly closed in sleep, but a few were staring into the center of the room, where three females were on their knees.

They were being questioned by two burly Kobalos warriors; two more watched from the side, smirking, obviously enjoying what was taking place.

What the women had done wrong, I never did discover. It might well have been part of their training: the Kobalos inflicted pain as an example to other slaves.

I floated up to the high ceiling of the chamber to watch. Suddenly one of the warriors struck a woman across the face with great force. Her head jerked back, and she groaned and began to sob.

"Be silent!" roared her attacker in Losta, the language of the Kobalos. "We inflict pain and you suffer, but you are not permitted to cry out or show that you are hurting. Do you understand?"

The woman continued to sob, and suddenly he drew a knife and cut her deeply on the forearm. She screamed, and blood began to seep from the deep wound.

The warrior's response was to hold the blade against her other arm. "I'll give you one more chance to be silent. Do you need a second cut from my blade?"

The woman stifled her cries as her blood dripped onto the floor. I was boiling with rage at such inhumane treatment; I would have liked nothing better than to slay her tormentor on the spot.

But if I were to do so, what then? If I killed these guards, all the women in this skleech pen would surely face reprisals. They would be tortured or slain.

So I watched and waited and endured the anguish of being a helpless witness to such barbarity. It was three hours before the guard was changed. I followed the four Kobalos out of the pen, eager to pay them back. I kept my distance as they walked down a series of dark passages, joking about what they had just done.

"Females are animals. Only through pain can they learn true obedience," one declared. His companions laughed and slapped him on the back.

Keeping close to the ceiling, I soared along the tunnel beyond them and took up my position at the next gateway, quickly returning to my human shape.

Then I drew my blades.

The nearest torch hung some distance away and the

entrance was in shadow, but perhaps they saw the light gleaming from my blades, because the four large warriors came to a sudden halt.

"This 'animal' is your death," I said quietly. "It is *your* turn to learn obedience. Come to me now, and die!"

The first one launched himself at me. He was faster than I'd expected, and agile for his size. But it availed him not. I deflected his blade and buried my own in his throat so that the blood that had given him life gushed out to splatter the wall and floor.

The other three attacked together. I could have killed them slowly, inflicting maximum pain to pay them back for what they had done to the women. But they posed no serious challenge. I finished it there and then, affording them the mercy of a quick death.

So far this had been easy, but I was under no illusion that it would always be so. These were just ordinary warriors; it would be a different matter to defeat a high mage or the Kobalos god, Talkus. Still, I'd tested my capabilities and strength, and all seemed satisfactory. My first venture had been successful, and I had learned much.

After replacing my blades in their scabbards, I retook the shape of an orb, sped through the stone walls, and soared into the dark sky to enter the purple tube of light.

Within moments I was walking back down the path, trees on either side of me. In the distance I could see the cauldron, where Thorne was waiting patiently.

"Did it go well?" she asked brightly as I approached.

"Very well. I will certainly be able to damage the Kobalos on my visits to Earth," I told her.

"And next time you will take me with you?"

I shook my head. "Not yet. There are skills that you must acquire in order to make movement back on Earth easier. I must teach you a shamanistic skill. You will need to be able to project your soul from your body; in the dead state I find myself in, I can shift shape instantly. If you are to accompany me, child, such a skill is vital. It makes it possible to pass through solid objects and move at great speed. In some situations, this may be the only way we can access the path back to the cauldron."

"Then teach me, Grimalkin. I am eager to learn!" Thorne cried.

So I began to teach her. If she could learn the skill, she could accompany me on my nocturnal visits. Two could accomplish far more than one.

However, in one respect my successful penetration of Valkarky had made me realize the limitations of what was possible. I wanted to hurt the Kobalos and damage their war effort, but my main ambition was to release the thousands of female slaves from the skleech pens and escort them to safety.

The fact that my visits to Earth could take place only during the hours of darkness made that impossible. Who would guide and protect them under the glare of the sun? I would need an army of living humans to help me.

If something was not done soon, the Kobalos would achieve their terrible goal. All human males would be dead; all the females would be slaves.

Tom Ward

14
The Increasing Threat

No sooner had I spoken the word "tulpa" than the entity that thought it was Bill Arkwright dropped the staff and sank to its knees on the edge of the mill stream, facing the waterwheel, its whole body shuddering. Then it twisted its head and looked up at me, face contorted with grief and pain.

"You are right," it cried, tears streaming from its eyes. "Now I know myself. I am a tulpa, the creation of a mage. Even a dog has more soul than me. I'm a thing without a soul. From nothing I came, and to nothing I will return!"

Then the face seemed to distort. The left eye drooped down the cheek, the jawbone stretched until it hung low on the chest, and the mouth began to drool a thick, slimy gray ribbon of saliva that puddled in the mud. I took a step back in horror and heard Jenny stifle a scream. I suddenly saw flecks of white in the saliva and realized that the creature's teeth were falling out.

The trembling of the body turned into violent convulsions. The thing that had mimicked Arkwright was crouched low, its forehead in the mud. It was moaning pitifully, its limbs writhing and twisting, the head becoming tubular and wormlike. Gray slime oozed from under its clothes and slid into the water, to be whirled away by the rush of the stream.

In less than a minute, nothing remained but empty garments. All that was left of the tulpa's flesh was the stench of rot.

Jenny and I left the waterwheel and went back to sit facing each other in the kitchen, stunned by what we'd just witnessed. Blood was sleeping fitfully; she kept twitching, as if troubled by bad dreams. We talked things through, trying to make sense of what had happened.

"You really think it was a tulpa?" Jenny asked, still trembling, her head in her hands.

I frowned. "It seemed to acknowledge the fact at the end. Didn't you hear what it said?"

I reached into my bag and pulled out the sheets of paper copied from the version of Nicholas Browne's glossary that I'd borrowed from Grimalkin. Browne had been a spook, and he'd once studied the Kobalos and left a guide to their customs, gods, magic, and behavior.

Grimalkin and I had added to that glossary as we learned new things, building our store of knowledge.

Jenny looked up as I skimmed down through the entries. I turned to the TULPA heading and handed the piece of paper to her, then stood up and read the entry over her shoulder. It consisted of the original Browne entry, followed by Grimalkin's comment, and then my own:

Tulpa: *A creature created within the mind of a mage and occasionally given form in the outer world.*

Note: I have traveled extensively and probed into the esoteric arts of witches and mages, but this is a magical skill that I have never encountered before. Are Kobalos mages capable of this? If so, their creatures may be limited only by the extent of their imaginations.—Grimalkin

Note: The winged being that spoke to the magowie and seemed to bring me back to life was a tulpa, created from the imagination of Alice. We have yet to encounter a tulpa created by the Kobalos, but we must be on our guard.—Tom Ward

I had once fought a Shaiksa assassin, but in the moment of victory, I had been slain, a saber passing right through my body. I still had scars to prove it—scales that covered the site of the wound, a legacy of the lamia blood I'd inherited from my mam. I'd died, but had been brought back to life by the power of Alice's magic. As I'd burst out of my coffin, an angel tulpa had appeared in the sky.

"According to Alice, the winged angel was a tulpa, but we've no proof that *this* creature was," Jenny observed. "We don't know enough about them. Maybe the thing just picked up on what you said, Tom. Maybe it just accepted your explanation. It had been having problems with its memory. It knew that things weren't right."

I nodded, taking the sheet of paper from her and carefully placing it, with the others, in my bag. "It does seem likely, though. What's interesting is that, at first, the tulpa really thought it was Bill Arkwright."

I'd experienced a real sense of loss when the entity melted away. It had been good to be in Arkwright's company again—I'd missed him. Now I was overcome by the feeling of sadness I'd felt when he died back in Greece.

"That's the *really* horrible thing about it," Jenny said. "It was alive and aware, and it died a horrible death knowing that was the end of it because it didn't have a soul. When you called it a tulpa, that's when it started to melt."

"Maybe naming it is what ends the spell that holds it together," I suggested. "It might have believed it was Bill Arkwright, which was why it didn't attack us at first. But there must have been some sort of trigger to make it understand its true purpose, to see us as enemies and go on the offensive."

"Maybe that would have happened when it had the Starblade in its possession," Jenny mused. "It asked to hold the sword, remember? I think its mission was to seize the Starblade and make you vulnerable to Kobalos magic. This thing was far more intricate than Alice's tulpa. Hers just kept its distance in the sky; it was perhaps more of an illusion than a creature with real substance. If this one was a tulpa, it was incredibly complex. It interacted with us for days. I wonder which mage created it. Maybe it was Balkai. Maybe he sent it."

We had yet to encounter this most powerful Kobalos mage, but it seemed likely that Jenny was right. It would have taken incredible magical skill to create such an entity.

"I think the best thing we can do is head back to Chipenden right now, while we've still got a few hours of daylight ahead of us," I said.

"It can't be soon enough for me. This place is creepy,"

Jenny said, rising to her feet and picking up her bag and staff.

We went into the front room with Blood at our heels, but when I opened the door she growled and lay down on her haunches, reluctant to go any farther. I clicked my tongue impatiently, and she finally came to her feet, shook herself, then followed us through the doorway into the mist.

I led the way through the garden toward the gap in the fence. The visibility was still deteriorating, and the air was cold and damp. It would be good to reach the canal and head south. But when we reached the moat, we came to a halt and stared across at the sight that awaited us there.

There was something sticking up out of the mist. It looked like a line of stakes set into the ground at forty-five degrees to repel attackers—but these were moving in unison. As we drew closer, we realized what they were.

Skelts!

Quivering on their multijointed legs, they moved like giant insects—though the segmented tubular bodies were hard and ridged like the shells of lobsters, and they were covered with barnacles that had attached themselves during the long periods they spent underwater.

Suddenly one of the skelts rushed forward to attack.

Jenny gave a cry and took a step back, but the creature came to a halt at the edge of the moat and crouched there, trembling, thwarted by the salt in the water.

These creatures were dangerous and could move incredibly quickly. I knew that there were too many for us to fight our way through. We were totally outnumbered. The only thing keeping those skelts at bay was that saltwater moat.

At my side, Blood began to whine and cower in fear. It was a sad thing to see: her spirit seemed to have been broken by her recent experiences.

I gestured with my staff and led Jenny and the dog back toward the mill. We needed to consider our options. We didn't have many, and none offered an easy exit from the mill garden.

Back in the kitchen, we sat in silence while I thought things through.

"Well, what do you think we should do about the skelt problem?" I asked Jenny.

"We could sit tight for a while. There are rabbit warrens in the far corner of the garden behind the mill. We wouldn't starve," she replied.

"But if it rains, as it often does in the County, the salt content of the moat will get diluted. After a while the skelts will be able to cross. We'd have a few days at most, Jenny. Then we'd have to face them. We'd just be delaying the inevitable."

"Couldn't you use a mirror and ask Alice for help? She'd sort them out. Remember what she did to the Kobalos army!"

With the aid of the Old God Pan, Alice had used her magic to cause a massive eruption of earth, which had destroyed part of the Kobalos army and allowed our rear guard to escape across the river to the human principality of Polyznia.

"I can't ask her to come here," I told Jenny. "She's trying to arrange an alliance with the Pendle witches. That's important. It may be all that stands between the County and the power of the Kobalos mages. No, we're going to wait for nightfall and then make a run for it."

"We'll never get past those skelts!" she cried.

"There *is* a way. Think about it. Imagine you're on your own and you have to escape. How would you do it?"

Jenny frowned, but suddenly her face lit up. "There's another way out! We could follow the course of the stream that runs under the fence and the moat."

"Well done!" I said. "That's exactly what we're going to do!"

The garden was surrounded by the moat, but it was also enclosed by a high iron fence. However, the millstream flowed through two tunnels that led under the moat. Across the mouths of these were iron grilles, allowing the water through but stopping anything from the dark from coming into the garden. Each grille was bolted to the stones that lined the tunnel. I'd need to remove it—a job that would have to be accomplished in daylight, for after dark I'd need a lantern to see what I was doing, and that would attract the attention of the skelts.

The tunnel that headed east out of the garden and emerged closest to the canal was our best option, I decided. I explained to Jenny what needed to be done, then headed for the workshop and selected some likely tools. While I did this, she started collecting pebbles and setting them down on the grass near the gap in the fence. When I emerged again, she was filling the pockets of her gown with the last batch. She looked dejected.

"See how many skelts you can hit!" I laughed, trying to cheer her up.

She nodded but didn't even raise a smile. I didn't blame her. We were in serious trouble.

The danger wasn't immediate, but the threat was still severe. If we didn't manage to escape, within days we would be dead. And there was no guarantee that there wouldn't be skelts lurking beyond the tunnel.

The plan was for Jenny to stand by the moat and hurl stones over the moat at the skelts. She'd be safe enough because they couldn't cross the salty water. It wouldn't do them any serious damage because of their hard shells, but I hoped it would distract them from what I was doing. Otherwise they might come around and enter the tunnel from the other end.

I walked rapidly beside the stream, stepped into the cold water, and splashed my way down the tunnel toward the iron grille. Luckily the stream wasn't deep here; it only came up to my knees. It was gloomy, but my eyes soon adjusted. One of the wrenches I'd brought seemed to be the right size, I thought.

I got down to work right away, but despite my best efforts the wrench kept slipping off the nuts. Each time that happened, there was a loud metallic clang; at one point the wrench caught the grille, and I thought the noise would surely give me away. I worked as quickly as I could. There were six nuts in all, and I had to get them off before the sun went down, when I would be forced to use a lantern. We needed to escape tonight—there was no guarantee that we'd survive another day. One heavy downpour might dilute the salt, and the skelts would cross the moat and attack.

The two remaining nuts lay below the surface and

were badly rusted. I was working just as fast as I could, but I made slow progress. The final nut was resisting all my efforts, but fortunately the stud snapped off and the nut fell into the water, still attached to it.

I'd succeeded, but it had taken me almost two hours. By the time I'd finished, I was shivering with cold. I headed over to where Jenny was still throwing stones and beckoned her back to the mill.

Inside, Blood was sleeping fitfully by the door. I fed wood into the stove and Jenny went to catch a couple of rabbits. She returned with only one, and we shared it with the dog, so we still felt hungry after our meal. However, dark came soon enough, and we prepared for our escape.

"Listen," I told Jenny. "The skelts may follow us. They're quick over short distances, but once we're clear, we can make good progress. We need to keep moving through the night and not let up until we're safely home."

"The sooner the better," Jenny agreed. "I certainly won't be dawdling."

"There could be other dangers from the dark out there. We might encounter Kobalos warriors brought here by their mages—or even Balkai himself. So we're not going to take the most direct route back to Chipenden. As soon as we leave the canal, we'll follow the ley lines."

"You plan to summon the boggart?" Jenny asked me.

"Yes, if there's no other option," I replied.

Ley lines were invisible routes that crossed the County; boggarts used them to move from place to place. I had a pact with Kratch, the boggart that defended the Chipenden garden: if summoned, it would come to my aid, but I needed to be on a ley line or within range of one of the intersection points.

"You've studied the maps, but how well do you know them?" I asked Jenny. "Are they fixed inside your memory? A spook needs to know the County like the back of his—or *her*—hand," I added with a smile. "So consider this to be part of your training. Try to work out the fastest route to Chipenden, making the best use of ley lines."

"I can only remember two of the major ones," Jenny said. "One runs northeast, passing through Leyland, Hoghton, and Billinge. But that's south of Priestown—nowhere near where we are now. If we were down there heading north, the second one would be more promising. It runs through Priestown, Goosnargh, Beacon Fell, and Bleasdale, ending up west of Chipenden."

"Well, that's good. You know two, but there are a lot more than that, and one lies quite close to where we are now. Keep thinking about it. It's time we were off. . . ."

We left the mill, locking the door behind us, and

followed the stream to the tunnel. I led the way and Jenny followed, but Blood stayed on the bank and started to whine softly. I clicked my tongue at her, but she didn't move. There was nothing I could do about it. If the dog had any sense, she would follow us.

Jenny was struggling to carry both our staffs and bags. I had the Starblade in my shoulder scabbard but needed both arms free so that I could lift the heavy iron grille out of the way. I went ahead into the darkness of the tunnel, gripped the iron lattice, and tugged it toward me. At first there was resistance. It had snagged on the studs—maybe they were bent. I tried again, and it jerked free with a loud clang of metal on stone that echoed down the tunnel. I leaned it against the left wall, leaving us just enough space to pass by.

I walked on into the tunnel and had an unpleasant surprise. The water suddenly became a lot deeper, almost reaching my waist. I gasped with cold and struggled on, with Jenny splashing along behind me. Moments later I was out of the tunnel and able to climb up onto the bank. It was still very misty, but I could see the gibbous moon overhead. As I turned and looked back to see if Jenny was all right, I heard a sound to my right.

Before I could react, a huge skelt came scuttling toward me, its joints creaking. I twisted aside and managed to avoid the point of its bone tube, but in doing so I overbalanced and fell heavily, knocking the wind from my lungs.

I came up onto my knees and reached for the Starblade as the skelt, ears flattened against its bony elongated head, darted in again.

My blood ran cold.

I had no time to draw my sword.

Grimalkin

15
What Dark Thing?

While I was teaching Thorne the skills she needed, the air shimmered in front of us and Pan appeared.

He was smiling. "I bear good tidings," he said. "Lukrasta lives!"

I gazed at him in astonishment. "Alice said that he was dead."

"We both believed that was so, but the Kobalos mages and their god, Talkus, are masters of deceit and illusion. It has taken me until now to penetrate their deception, and we are only just in time to save him. Soon he truly is to be put to death. What better test of your new powers than to rescue the mage? We badly need his magical strength."

Lukrasta was the most powerful human mage who had ever walked the Earth. He would no doubt be a useful addition to our forces, but I did not trust him. He cared only for power. Would he expect to work closely with Alice again? Would this mean that Pan would ask Alice to abandon Tom once more?

If that was the case, I felt sorry for Tom Ward, but this was not the time to debate such matters. I knew that I must put aside my own concerns and work for the greater good. To defeat the Kobalos, we would need all the help we could get.

Thorne and I headed back toward the cauldron.

"Please take me with you, Grimalkin!" Thorne begged me again.

"You are not yet ready, child. I cannot do so until you have learned those skills. This will be very dangerous. To reach Lukrasta, I will need to become an orb and pass through solid stone. That is something you cannot yet do," I told her, frowning.

She hung her head, and soon the paths were spinning and I was walking toward Valkarky once again, concentrating on the exact spot where I needed to be.

I felt that lurch in my stomach, as if I was falling, and then an intense feeling of nausea and cold. But the pain was much less severe than it had been on the previous occasion. Perhaps Hecate had exaggerated it. Maybe I would grow accustomed to the sensation.

Instinctively I closed my eyes. When I opened them again, I was standing in a narrow stone corridor. To right and left were doors that led into the cells. This time the purple tube lay at ground level. I would be able to simply walk into it. But what of others, such as Kobalos mages? Could they do the same? I wondered. Or would it be barred to them, or perhaps hidden from their sight?

Every twenty paces, wall torches lit the passageway. However, I was a creature of the dark and so had to use darkness to my advantage. I exerted my will and snuffed out all the torches within sight, plunging the area into gloom.

I could still see; everything was outlined with green edges—though I could also make out a flicker of yellow torchlight from the third door on the left.

I glanced up and down the corridor; it was still deserted. Wasting no time, I headed for the cell, where I sensed the presence of Lukrasta. I concentrated, transforming the substance of my being and shifting my shape into that of a small orb, then floated through the solid wooden door.

I changed back into my human shape and gazed about me. For a moment I could make no sense of what I saw.

The large cell was lit by a torch fastened to the far wall. It reminded me of a blacksmith's shop: in the near corner by the door stood a glowing brazier. I could feel its heat as I entered. The walls were hung with an assortment of tools: axes, blades, tongs, hammers, and saws. There were also chains hanging from the ceiling and a large anvil.

It was a torture chamber.

When I stepped farther in, passing beyond the warmth of the brazier, I felt the damp chill in the air and smelled tar. Suddenly I noticed that some of the tools were stained with blood; there were dark patches of it on the dank stone walls, and a large pool on the flags. Equally ominous was the executioner's block that stood there.

Where was Lukrasta? I wondered. Was I too late? Had he already been killed?

Then I noticed, in the shadows beyond the candle flame in the far corner of the cell, what I at first took for a bundle of dirty, crumpled rags. I stepped nearer and realized that it was someone chained with his back to the wall, head slumped forward onto his chest so that his face was in darkness.

It was Lukrasta.

His hands had been amputated and the stumps were black—caked with tar to staunch the bleeding and prevent infection. Whoever had done this wanted to keep him alive for further torture. It must have been agonizing to have your hands chopped off and your arms plunged into hot tar. The shock would have killed most men, but he had been strong.

Studying him more closely, I realized that this was no longer the case. He was emaciated, the flesh wasted, the bones protruding.

"Lukrasta!" I called, and he looked up, revealing his face to the candlelight. He had the same long mustache, but it was stained with blood and there were streaks on his chin. His lips had been stitched together.

He appeared bewildered, and stared at me, his eyes widening, looking like a madman. Could he have been driven insane by what he had suffered, or was it just confusion at my unexpected presence in his cell? No doubt, as one of the dead revisiting the Earth, I was terrifying to behold.

Then I saw the marks on Lukrasta's neck: a variety of scars—some old, others very recent. One was a red hole still dribbling blood and fluid. They had been draining him. Was that part of the torture, or a means of finding out about his capabilities?

Well, he was still alive, but I wondered if it was too late to make use of him. How could this shadow help us in our struggle against Talkus and his mages?

One by one, I snapped the chains that bound him at the neck, legs, and body. While I worked, Lukrasta stared at me, his eyes wild. He tried to speak, but he sounded like a wounded animal. Whether it was an attempt to tell me something or an expression of anguish, I couldn't tell. So I used one of my short blades to cut the stitching and free his lips.

"What dark thing are you?" he cried, his face twisting in terror. I knew then that his cry had been one of fear.

By way of answer, I snuffed out the torch on the wall and drained the brazier of heat so that in seconds it was filled with cold ashes.

Then I turned and approached him.

"I am Grimalkin!" I hissed into his ear. "Be silent while I remove you from this place!"

I helped him to his feet, but his whole body was shaking, and he hardly had the strength to stand. I knew that guards might arrive at any minute, so, wasting no more time, I hefted him over my shoulder in the manner of a spook carrying a witch, legs to the front. He was surprisingly light.

I could pass through the solid door, but he could not. Now that I had completed the more difficult part of my task—locating Lukrasta in his cell—I was no longer concerned about alerting enemies to my presence. I could fight my way to safety. I struck the door hard with the palm of my hand, reducing it to splinters.

I stepped through the gap carrying my burden out into the corridor. The noise brought guards running through the darkness, but unfortunately for them, they lay between me and the portal. It was easy to despatch them. They never saw their death coming.

Still carrying Lukrasta, the blade in my left hand dripping blood, I passed through the purple portal and returned to the dark.

Tom Ward

16
The Water Witch

I thought that my very last moment on Earth had come.

But before the skelt could reach me, something hit it hard, sending it flying.

It was Blood, the wolfhound.

Now the skelt lay on its back, its eight multijointed legs waving in the air. The dog was bravely trying to get a grip on the creature's throat, but was in danger from the legs, which were trying to close about her. Wasting no time, I came to my feet and drew the Starblade. The skelt's body had two segments; I struck with all my strength at the point where they joined.

The sword sliced right through the hard shell, cutting the creature in two. Its front part convulsed as the wolfhound tore at its throat, blood spraying over both of them.

Jenny came running to my side, eyes wide and fearful.

I returned the Starblade to its scabbard, then took my staff and bag from her. I clicked my tongue at Blood, and she came to my side obediently.

"Good dog!" I said, patting her head as she licked the skelt blood from her jaws. She had overcome her former nervousness and had just saved my life.

I looked at Jenny. "There could be other skelts nearby. We need to move fast!" I told her, heading along the stream toward the canal. Most of the creatures were probably still clustered around the gap in the fence; maybe a few were circling the boundary, but with luck the one we'd just killed was the only one. We had a chance to escape.

Soon we were scrambling up the slope onto the west bank of the canal. We hurried south along the towpath, our feet crunching on the cinders. I knew that there was a ley line that ran parallel with the canal several miles to the east. It would have been safer to follow that. However, its route led across farm ditches and fences. That would make for slow progress. The canal was faster, and for the first part of our journey I was relying on speed to get us clear of the skelts that might even now be in pursuit.

Up here on the canal bank, which was higher than the fields on either side, the mist was so thick that I couldn't see more than three or four feet in front of me. But above our heads, all was clear; I could see the moon and stars.

There was little chance of getting clear of the mist until we were well east of Caster, farther from the sea. I was striding along at a furious pace when suddenly I heard a scream and then a bark behind me.

Alarmed, I turned and saw Jenny struggling desperately. She'd fallen over, and one of her legs was in the water. Blood was at her side, growling at something in the canal, and Jenny was jabbing into the water with her staff; she looked terrified.

As I reached her side, I saw the hand that gripped her ankle; the sharp talons told me immediately that it was a water witch. The creature's face lay just below the surface of the water, long hair writhing like tentacles, predatory eyes glaring up at me.

These creatures had once been human females, but over long ages had become more like beasts. They were more instinctive than rational, and incredibly ferocious and strong. They could drag you down into the water and drain your blood before you'd even had time to drown. Or they could flay your skin and open you up to the bone, severing your limbs as rapidly as Grimalkin with her snippy scissors.

Jenny was struggling to keep the witch at bay with her staff. The dog was trying to help, but Jenny's ankle and the witch's taloned hand were underwater.

In this situation, rowan staffs were the most suitable weapons. I took mine in both hands, released the blade, and jabbed hard at the witch's face. Jenny was moaning with pain but still continued to stab down toward the witch. One of our blades must have cut the creature, because within seconds the water had begun to darken with blood, and she released the girl and swam away.

I dragged Jenny clear and quickly knelt to examine her ankle. To my dismay, the skin was broken in two different places where the witch had gripped her.

Wounds from water witches could easily become infected. Had Alice been here, she'd simply have used her herbs to ward off harm. However, looking more closely, I saw that Jenny's wound wasn't deep, so I cleaned away the beads of blood as best I could.

"Are you all right to continue?" I asked, helping her to her feet. "Do you need to rest for a while?"

She frowned. "I'd like to keep moving, but do we have to stay close to the canal?" she asked. "The witch might come back. It could be waiting ahead of us. Maybe there are others."

"I *was* going to follow the canal almost as far as Caster, but I've changed my mind. You're right. It's far too dangerous. We'll cross at the next bridge and head east toward the ley line."

There was no doubt in my mind that the skelts had been used against us by our Kobalos enemies. I wasn't sure about the water witch. They always lurked near water—having your ankle grabbed by a water witch was one of the routine hazards of walking the towpaths of this area. But gods, demons, and other entities from the dark were no doubt aligning themselves under the rule of Talkus. It was better to leave the canal now, just in case that applied to the County water witches as well; more could arrive at any minute.

There were lots of bridges across the canal, and we were soon able to reach the far bank and then follow a farm track that led eastward. After five minutes we were approaching the farm, and dogs started to bark in the distance. However, Blood was well trained and didn't respond.

We skirted the barn and farmhouse and took to the fields, our pace slowing. Sometimes we were able to climb gates or use a stile, but more often than not we were forced to negotiate a fence or struggle through a hedgerow.

My next task was to judge when we'd reached the ley line—at which point we would follow it south. Such lines passed through churches, standing stones, and other markers. For example, the second one that Jenny had mentioned, which ran approximately north-south through churches in Priestown and Goosnargh, also passed through Chingle Hall, which had a reputation for being the most haunted house in the County. Strange things happened on ley lines. However, the lines were invisible, so my best bet was to spot a church spire above the low mist.

I was grateful now that my master, John Gregory, had drummed into me the importance of knowing the landscape of the County. Under his direction I'd spend hours studying the maps. My knowledge of the locality told me that the church of St. Michael's should soon come into view. Sure enough, I spotted its tower to the northeast.

"What direction are we heading in, Jenny?" I asked.

"East," she replied promptly.

"How do you know that?"

"Because *you* told me that's the direction we were taking!" she exclaimed cheekily. "But I can also tell that by the position of the stars."

"Yes, they tell us that we are still heading east. So once St. Michael's church tower is directly on our left, we'll turn right and go south. It's a crude alignment, but it's the best I can do. Even if we're not actually walking the line, we'll be somewhere near it, and if I have to summon Kratch, he'll find us or guide us toward him."

We were soon heading south as I'd described. I turned to Jenny and asked her, "How are you feeling now?"

"My ankle's throbbing, but I've felt worse," she replied.

We continued on through the night. At dawn I called a halt for ten minutes. We were hungry, but all I had was some crumbly County cheese. Normally Jenny would have turned up her nose at it, but she ate her share without a word of complaint. The poor dog would be hungry, but I couldn't allow her to hunt in case she attracted attention.

We stood there, munching, unable to sit down because the ground was so soggy. We hunched together under a hawthorn hedge, close to a stagnant ditch full of muddy water.

"Where are we now?" Jenny asked.

"Somewhere to the northeast of Caster, but we're taking the long way round. As I said, following ley lines isn't always the fastest route to a destination."

"Well, at least the mist is clearing now," she commented.

Looking around, I saw that it was starting to lift and thin. In the gray morning light I could see halfway across the small field. Trees were starting to appear out of the gloom, their leafless branches like monstrous grasping arms. There was not the slightest breeze. Nothing was moving.

Suddenly from within the ditch came a flash of light. I stepped closer and, peering down into the gray water, saw that a small area, hardly larger than the palm of my hand, was brighter than the rest. It brightened further, and an image quickly began to form.

It was Alice's face.

My heart leaped in happiness at the sight of those beautiful brown eyes staring up at me, though her expression was very serious. There was no hint of a smile of greeting.

Witches used mirrors to communicate over long distances, but only the most powerful could use the surface of water in this way. Not only that—Alice had somehow known precisely where I was.

She began to mouth her message. There was no sound, but by now I was good at reading her lips.

It was not good news.

"Ain't safe to go back to Chipenden, Tom. They're lying in wait for you. Come to Pendle and fight with us. Kobalos mages and warriors have attacked and burned Goldshaw Booth. We've taken refuge in Malkin Tower. We'll make a stand there. Join us, please. I miss you, Tom."

Things sounded bad. Goldshaw Booth was the village of the Malkins, who were the most powerful of the Pendle clans, and yet they'd been unable to defend it. Was it just the Malkins who had taken refuge in the tower, or had they admitted the other clans as well? I wondered. Had Alice managed to secure the alliance of the Pendle witches that she'd sought? Their combined magic would be needed to counter the power of the Kobalos mages. I wondered how big a Kobalos force was in the area.

I realized that Alice was in terrible danger—I needed to reach that tower as soon as possible. I couldn't bear the thought of anything happening to her. If the witches had been forced to retreat, the enemy must have powerful mages with them . . . perhaps even Balkai, the most powerful member of the triumvirate.

I knelt down close to the patch of shining water, intending to question Alice, but I didn't get the chance. Her face had already faded from view.

"What did Alice say?" Jenny asked, frowning down into the ditch.

I came to my feet and told her. "We're heading directly for Pendle," I added, beginning to pace up and down nervously, my insides churning with anxiety at the thought that Alice might be in danger.

"They'll be lying in wait for us there too!" Jenny

exclaimed. "But now there'll be even more of them."

"Maybe, but I know Pendle well. We'll find a way to avoid them."

"Alice must know exactly where we are, or she couldn't have done that," Jenny said, pointing at the ditch. "How else could she have found us? If she knows, then there's a good chance the Kobalos mages will too—especially Balkai. We'll never reach that tower."

"There's a secret tunnel that leads into the tower," I told her. "I've used it before, more than once."

"But will it still be secret?"

I stared at Jenny and took a deep breath to calm myself. "Let's hope so," I said with a smile. She'd made a valid point: that tunnel might be unsafe now. The Kobalos mages might already have found it. They could ambush us there.

However, I was determined to go to Pendle. I needed to help Alice, whatever the cost.

Summoning the boggart Kratch to aid us might be a problem now. The route along the ley line was not the most direct one to Malkin Tower.

"We're going to continue south, Jenny, and pass to the west of Chipenden, picking up that ley line you mentioned earlier. It runs south through Beacon Fell, heading toward Priestown. But we'll leave it well before then. At

Goosnargh village, we'll head directly east along another one. That will bring us close to Pendle."

"Every step we take will bring us closer to danger," Jenny said, a frown on her face. "I've a bad feeling about this."

I didn't reply. She was right, of course, but I had no choice.

Grimalkin

17
Burning Light

Thorne was squatting on the ground beside Hecate's cauldron, eyes closed, brow furrowed in concentration. She was desperately trying to project her soul out of her body—so far, with little success.

I heard the beat of wings and drew a blade as three ravens landed on the branch overhead. They perched there and studied me.

I selected another blade, this time a throwing knife, but Thorne grabbed my arm.

"They are watchers, Grimalkin," she explained. "Entities able to search the Earth and report back on what they find."

"But these are the ones that served Hecate," I said, wondering how they felt about those who had slain their mistress.

"We serve she who controls the cauldron!" rasped a

harsh, raucous voice from above our heads—though the words were clear enough.

"Then you serve me," I said.

"We have tidings. We have seen danger to the spook called Ward, he who is your ally."

"Then tell me what you know," I commanded, returning my blades to their sheaths.

"He is heading south with his apprentice and they are approaching Beacon Fell, but Shaiksa assassins lie in ambush. One will challenge him, while the other three will attack him from behind with arrows. There is little time to lose. To save him you must intervene, but such an act will bring you into great danger."

"I do not fear Kobalos assassins!" I stated angrily.

"The danger to you is from a more formidable foe—the fierce heat of the sun," rasped the raven. "It is almost dawn."

I realized that I needed to intervene now, or Tom Ward would be slain. For long years we had striven together against the dark. And now, with his courage, experience—and the Starblade I had forged for him—Tom was a powerful ally we could not afford to lose.

But I could not survive the sun's rays.

On arriving, I crouched with my head touching the trunk of a tree. My insides twisted; my blood felt like it was boiling—but I could not afford to wait until I recovered. There was no cloud, and through the trees I could see that the sky on the eastern horizon was orange. The sun would rise in a matter of minutes.

I felt confident that I could slay the assassins . . . but could I do so in the limited time available to me?

I shifted into an orb and soared through the trees. Soon, below me, I saw the Shaiksa assassin. The watcher had used the word "ambush," but the Shaiksa was standing out in the open, ready to issue a challenge. He was there to avenge the brother assassin who Tom had slain on the riverbank.

His presence was a serious threat, though I felt sure that Tom would defeat him. But where were the other three assassins?

I searched the surrounding area until I found them.

They were hidden among the branches of separate trees, set in a triangle. As the watcher had indicated, their weapons were bows and arrows. When Tom went forward to fight the assassin, those archers would be behind him. They would shoot him in the back.

It was a treacherous plan. I had considered the Shaiksa brotherhood to be honorable. This showed how desperate they were: they feared Tom and were not confident of a victorious outcome. The Shaiksas comprised the foremost warriors available to the Kobalos; they always avenged a death. However, in Tom they had come up against a formidable adversary. They simply needed to be rid of him and snuff out the danger to the Kobalos cause. This time they would be sure of victory.

I glided toward the nearest of the three concealed assassins. I needed to strike swiftly and silently, lest I alert the others. Seconds later I had transformed into my human shape and straddled the branch directly behind the archer. I slayed him quickly with my blade, then repositioned his dead body carefully upon the branch with his bow on his back so that it would not fall out of the tree. I knew that in death he would contact his brothers, but I needed to buy a little time before I found the second of the Shaiksas.

I returned my blade to its sheath and prepared to deal with my next enemy. But first I glanced toward the horizon.

It was brighter. The sun would be rising at any moment.

The second assassination was not so straightforward. With his dying breath, the first Shaiksa would have sent out the news of his death—though he could not identify his slayer; he had been dispatched too quickly.

My second target was vigilant and saw me take shape

behind him. Still, I clamped my hand over his mouth so that he could not cry out. I slayed him also and then prepared to deal with the third bowman.

This Shaiksa was actually standing on a branch, his eyes wide, searching for a target and drawing his bow. I attacked him head-on, but the moment I dashed his bow aside and raised my blade I felt a terrible flash of burning light in my face. The sun had come up.

Now, for the first time since reaching the dark, my fear returned. I dreaded losing my vision. Without sight, how could I function as an assassin?

I felt my face begin to bubble and blister. Hot, burning tears ran down my cheeks. Were my eyes melting? I thought fearfully.

I was in agony.

I was blind.

Tom Ward

18
A Shaiksa with a Bow

We had been following the new ley line, heading toward Beacon Fell. I could see its forested slopes in the distance. The sky was clear, and the first hint of dawn light showed directly ahead in the east.

Ahead lay a wood—a likely place for our enemies to lurk and ambush us. I considered making a detour and following its western edge. However, that would mean leaving the ley line, and I might still need to summon the boggart.

So, leading the way, I strode on into the trees. Five minutes later, just as the sun rose, lighting the treetops, we reached a clearing. Immediately I saw danger waiting at its center: an armed and armored figure, with the three pigtails that marked him as a Shaiksa assassin.

This was no ambush. It was an open challenge.

"They'll never give up!" Jenny cried in alarm.

Each dying assassin called out with his mind to summon the Shaiksa brotherhood to avenge his death. I had killed an assassin on the riverbank back in Polyznia; I had fought the second Shaiksa that Alice had slain with her dagger. Moreover, I had led an army across the Shanna River into their territory. No doubt they considered me a threat that must be removed once and for all. Jenny was right: their vengeful pursuit of me would never end. They would be satisfied only when I was dead.

Blood growled and began to move forward, her fur standing on end, saliva dripping from her jaws. I clicked my tongue, and she halted and looked back at me. Had she been human, I'd have judged her expression to be one of disappointment.

"Look after the dog, Jenny. Blood has no chance against such an opponent. He'd just cut her to pieces," I said.

"Summon the boggart, Tom! Don't risk your life again," Jenny pleaded, placing her hand on Blood's back to restrain her.

"I think I should save the boggart for something worse," I said, putting down my bag and laying my staff beside it. "I should be able to deal with this."

"Worse? What could be worse than fighting that killer? Remember what happened last time. You could die again, but this time you wouldn't come back!" Jenny cried.

I didn't reply. There was nothing to be said. I'd already made up my mind to fight. It would be a fair contest, and I was confident I could win.

I removed my cloak to allow myself more freedom of movement, and then I reached up to the shoulder scabbard and drew the Starblade. Gripping it two-handed, I strode toward my opponent.

The Shaiksa's armor was black and of the highest quality, plate laid across plate so as not to allow the slightest point of vulnerability. Around his neck he wore a bone necklace. Grimalkin, the witch assassin, had always worn a necklace of thumb bones; within each one lay the stored magical power of its dead owner—a resource she could draw on if necessary. From *this* necklace hung the shrunken skulls of the Shaiksa's defeated enemies. They contained no magic: this was a boast, a kill count; a display of prowess. No doubt his intention was that my own skull should join them.

The assassin wore no helmet. I could see his lupine face and pitiless eyes. This was surely a vulnerable point to keep in mind. He stared at me arrogantly, a saber gripped in each hand.

When I stood about six feet from him, I heard a noise

behind me and whirled around to see that Jenny had followed me.

"Go back!" I commanded, giving her a slight push and sending her reeling backward. "You can't help me. Stay out of danger!"

I expected her to protest, but she nodded and backed away, her expression fearful.

I took another couple of steps toward the Shaiksa, then halted, preferring to let him attack first. In defending myself, I could assess his strengths and weaknesses and determine how best to defeat him.

But could I really defeat such an assassin again? I wondered now. Suddenly Jenny's suggestion about the boggart seemed like a good idea. But then I remembered what Grimalkin had said to me after my defeat of Lenklewth, the Kobalos high mage.

It was as if her voice was speaking those words inside my head:

"I think the Starblade is growing in strength. That is another of the features I built into it. The blade will absorb from you what you are and what you are becoming."

Yes! I *could* do it again. The long illness I'd suffered after my apparent death on the riverbank belonged to the past. I was fully recovered. My strength and my speed had both fully returned. Without further thought I pushed caution aside, seized the initiative, and attacked.

The assassin blocked my first blow with his left saber and lunged at me with his right, but I danced away and began to spin, moving forward to attack again, performing the dance of death that Grimalkin had taught me.

My anger began to grow, but it was not like a red mist of berserker fury, limiting my ability to think and fight tactically. To fight that way was always a mistake. *This* anger was a fuel that surged through my body to feed my speed and strength. *How dare this Shaiksa assassin confront me here in the County, my home?* I thought indignantly. What right had this invader to block my way to Pendle, standing between me and Alice?

It was my rusty sword against his glittering sabers. But the Starblade that I held contained the best of Grimalkin's magic. It would not break and could cut through any armor. Grimalkin was dead, but this was her legacy, and I would use it to good effect. Still gripping the Starblade with both hands, I scythed with all my force from right to left.

The sword bit deep into the assassin's left shoulder, cutting through his armor, and he staggered backward. He still held both sabers, but the one in his left hand hung low, pointing to the ground. There was blood running down his arm and spraying onto the grass.

Wasting no time, I pressed home my advantage, attacking his left side again. He was unable to raise the saber to parry my blade, and it inflicted a second wound just below the first. This time the assassin dropped the saber, but before it reached the ground I'd spun the other way and cut him deeply, high on his right shoulder.

He began to retreat; I darted after him, slicing through his armor again and again. Finally I forced him back against the trunk of a tree, raining down blow after blow, each taking its toll. I don't know which blow finally killed him, but within seconds he was lying sprawled at my feet.

I stood looking down at him, fighting to regain my breath. I was hardly aware of Jenny coming to my side. When I glanced at her, she was staring across the clearing and pointing out a tree to our right.

"There's a body lying in the grass over there," she said.

We went over and saw another Shaiksa assassin lying dead at our feet. His throat had been cut; his bow lay nearby.

"Who could have killed him?" Jenny asked, glancing about as if expecting to see someone else.

I shook my head. There was no way to know. I'd never seen a Shaiksa with a bow before. Had this been an ambush after all? Had they intended to slay me from a distance or as I fought?

"Are we going to bury the bodies?" Jenny asked, glancing back at the assassin I'd slain.

I shook my head. "In other circumstances I would, but it's dangerous to linger here. In any case, in death he'll have told his brother assassins what happened and where he is. They'll come for him."

So we pressed on through the morning. Late in the afternoon, we rested in another wood within a mile of Goosnargh. We needed to reach the center of the village and follow the ley line east.

Jenny caught rabbits to feed us and the dog, and then we slept for a while. I felt confident that Blood would wake us if anybody approached. The real Bill Arkwright had trained her well.

We set off again about an hour after sunset and headed toward the village.

It was then that I noticed that Jenny was limping. "Is that ankle bothering you?" I asked her.

"Yes, it's starting to feel a bit sore—but don't worry, I can still walk."

"Let me see. . . ."

I knelt and looked at her ankle. The moon was hidden by clouds and the light wasn't good, but her skin felt hot to the touch, the joint swollen. I'd worried about the cuts from the water witch's talons; they had indeed become infected. Such wounds could be very dangerous.

I didn't want to alarm Jenny, so I simply led the way toward the village more slowly. Soon it was in sight.

"There's something wrong, Tom," Jenny warned, taking my arm to bring me to a halt.

She was right. No lights showed from any of the dwellings—but surely most people would not yet be in bed. Everything was too quiet, and now I could smell smoke.

I put my forefinger to my lips to indicate the need for silence, and then we moved forward more cautiously, Blood padding at our side. We'd almost reached the first cottage when the moon came out from behind a cloud, flooding the scene with silver light.

I saw several things simultaneously, and quickly pulled Jenny into the shadow of a wall.

Most of the houses had no roofs; some had only two or three walls still standing. They were burned empty shells. In the center of the village green was a large mound. At first my eyes refused to accept what I was seeing, but then a sudden breeze carried a second smell toward us—one even stronger than the smoke.

It was the stink of death.

Ahead of us lay a mound of corpses. The villagers had all been slain.

Then, beyond the mound, I saw a bulky figure pacing back and forth as if on sentry duty. The moon glinted off his chain mail, and I realized that it was a Kobalos warrior.

We began to retreat, keeping to the shadows. I knew that more of our enemies would be lurking nearby.

We could avoid a dangerous confrontation here, but it involved a change of plan. Now we would have to circle Goosnargh and, in so doing, leave the ley line. Who could tell how many Kobalos were in the vicinity? It would be dangerous to head east, but there was a second ley line that led toward Pendle. We needed to press on south toward it. This was the ley line that bisected the notorious, haunted Chingle Hall.

We got clear of Goosnargh without encountering any more Kobalos, still heading south. Jenny's limp seemed to be getting worse. She kept giving little gasps of pain. Blood started to sniff at her ankle, whining softly.

"Do you want to rest for a while?" I asked, taking Jenny's arm to bring her to a halt.

"No, let's keep going," she said.

But as we continued our journey, I grew increasingly

worried. If only Alice was here, she'd have something to counter the poison. Once we reached Pendle she'd be able to help, but now I doubted that my apprentice could walk that far.

Suddenly Jenny gave a little cry and fell onto her knees. When I reached her, she was panting for breath.

"Sorry, Tom. Sorry. Sorry. Sorry . . ."

Then she pitched forward onto her face. I turned her onto her side. She was now unconscious, her breathing ragged, and her ankle was terribly swollen. The poison was spreading rapidly, and I was full of fear. What could I do? How could I help her?

I lifted her onto my shoulder and strode on as fast as I could. As well as carrying Jenny, I was struggling with both bags and staffs.

Fortunately I hadn't far to walk. Chingle Hall lay not far ahead. I could stop there and ask for help.

I'd visited the place on several occasions with my master. At Squire Robinson's request, John Gregory had sent several of its ghosts to the light, though others had kept manifesting themselves.

But of more interest to me now was the fact that one of the servants had some medical knowledge. This was usually the case with big houses belonging to the gentry. Such skill could mean the difference between life and death. Sometimes it could take hours for a doctor to arrive.

The servant's name was Nora, and she knew all about herbs; not as much as Alice, of course, but it had to be worth a try. I couldn't think of anything else and was growing increasingly desperate. I just had to hope that she was still working there. I knew that people had died as a result of water-witch poison.

19
Chingle Hall

It was set within a tangle of trees; it looked gloomy and forbidding. However, I was encouraged by the sight of lights shining from two of the downstairs windows. The house was occupied and the inhabitants hadn't yet retired for the night.

I hoped that Squire Robinson was at home. He was a strong-willed, level-headed person who hadn't allowed himself to be frightened by ghosts or driven from his home. He also knew me by sight—which would speed up the process of getting help for Jenny.

I placed the bags and staffs on the step and deposited Jenny carefully so that she was leaning against the wall. Then I rapped hard on the door. After a few moments' delay, I heard approaching footsteps, and the bolts were drawn back.

The door opened and I found myself face-to-face with

a tall, thin, hatchet-faced servant. She looked me up and down with obvious contempt.

"I am Mrs. Hesketh, Squire Robinson's housekeeper. My master is away," she said in an imperious voice. "How *dare* you come knocking at our front door! The tradesmen's entrance is at the side of the house."

Then she stared down at Blood as if she intended to kick her—not an advisable course of action. The wolfhound glared up at her and gave a low growl.

Strictly speaking, I *was* a tradesman: spook's business was a craft. And some titled and well-to-do people expected tradesmen such as butchers, grocers, carpenters, and the like to use that side entrance. The rule was often enforced by snobbish servants rather than those who employed them. Squire Robinson had always received my master and me with courtesy, and we'd been admitted through the front door. Now that he was away, the rules were clearly different.

"My apprentice is very ill," I said, gesturing toward Jenny. "She's been poisoned. I'd like to see Nora, please. I'm hoping that she can help. This is an emergency."

"Round the side!" Mrs. Hesketh snapped, and slammed the door in my face.

I picked up Jenny, along with the bags and staffs, and trudged round to the side door, which was a long time opening.

"You may enter, but first wipe your dirty feet on the mat!" the housekeeper ordered.

I stamped off the mud, then carried Jenny over the threshold.

"The dog stays outside!" Mrs. Hesketh snapped.

I pointed down. "Stay, Blood!" I commanded, and watched her settle herself outside the door.

As the housekeeper slammed it behind us, I looked about me. The small, chilly, flagged hallway was windowless, its only item of furniture a bench set against the wall. No doubt tradesmen were kept waiting there at Mrs. Hesketh's pleasure.

Suddenly a feeling of cold ran up and down my spine, the warning a seventh son of a seventh son receives when something from the dark is nearby. There were clearly new ghosts to be dealt with here, but that would have to wait until another time.

"You may stay until Nora returns," the housekeeper told me. "She's out gathering herbs." She gave me another glance of disdain, then turned and left.

I carefully placed Jenny on her side on the hard bench, then took off my cloak to make a pillow for her head. She kept gasping, as if struggling to draw breath, and her forehead was hot with fever. I quickly examined her ankle again; I didn't like what I saw. Now, in addition to the swelling, purple veins extended up her leg almost as far as the knee.

I just hoped that Nora could help. She had a reputation as a skilled healer; my master had once told me that he suspected she was a benign witch. The fact that she'd gone out after dark to collect herbs confirmed the idea in my mind. Some believed that herbs and roots gathered under the light of the moon had greater potency. It gave me hope that she might be able to help Jenny.

At first I paced up and down impatiently, awaiting her return; then weariness began to overtake me. I sat down on the bench, my right knee almost touching Jenny's head, and fought to stay awake. My eyes kept closing, but at the point of sleep I would jerk back to wakefulness.

All at once something changed. In my drowsy state I couldn't work out what it was. Then I knew.

It was too quiet . . . Jenny was no longer breathing!

I shook her gently by the shoulders. At first she didn't respond; then, suddenly, she drew in a shuddering breath, but it was a long time before she took another. She was still alive, but her breathing had become very irregular.

Where was Nora? I wondered desperately. Why was she so long?

Then, in the distance, I thought I heard a dog barking. Opening the door to check on Blood, I saw that she'd gone. I was surprised that she'd wandered off like that after I'd clearly told her to remain there. Dogs trained by Bill Arkwright were always very obedient. What could have caused her to stray?

I closed the door and sat down beside Jenny again, her erratic breathing making me increasingly nervous. Not long after, I heard footsteps outside, the door opened, and Nora came in, carrying a small canvas bag full of herbs.

She was exactly as I remembered from my last visit to the hall: a short, chubby, motherly woman with red cheeks, a kind face, and graying hair.

"What's this? What's this?" she cried, coming to Jenny's side and laying a hand upon her feverish brow.

I explained quickly what had happened.

"We need to get her into bed. I'll have to ask Mrs. Hesketh's permission," she said, bustling through the inner door and closing it behind her.

Nora was away for some time, and I started to get impatient. What was keeping her? Then she returned, holding the door open.

"Bring her through!" she cried. "She can have my room."

Carrying Jenny, I followed Nora down the corridor to the servants' quarters. The room was small—just a single bed, a chair, and a small chest for clothes. I carefully placed Jenny on the bed and sat there holding her hand. Nora returned a few moments later with a bowl of water and a sponge, and gently bathed Jenny's face, then examined her ankle.

Once she'd finished, she looked up at me. Her expression was bleak.

"You must be the new spook—I heard that old John Gregory had passed away. I remember you coming here. You were a skinny little thing. You've shot up like a beanstalk since then!" she said.

"Jenny is my first apprentice. Can you help her?" I asked.

"I've got herbs simmering now, but I fear it may be too late," Nora said, shaking her head. "The poison's spreading up her body toward her heart. I'll do my best, though, never you fear . . . while there's life there's always hope."

Her words filled me with dismay. In trying to press on toward Malkin Tower, I'd taken a risk. I knew now that I should have taken Jenny for help immediately after the attack. My heart felt heavy.

I watched as Nora tried to get Jenny to swallow the infusion of herbs. The girl choked and spluttered, and most of the liquid ended up on the pillow. I began to feel more and more desperate.

Suddenly I smelled an odor, faint but definite—the scent of flowers of a type I couldn't put a name to. I realized that it came from Jenny, and I remembered where and when I'd smelled it before: early in my apprenticeship I'd visited the farm when Dad was very ill, and I'd smelled that same strange scent in his room.

I'd mentioned it to Mam, and she told me that it was a manifestation of one of the gifts I'd inherited, not because I was a seventh son of a seventh son, but from her. I later learned that Mam was the first lamia. She called the gift "intimations of death." It seemed to me more like a curse than a gift. When you met someone who exuded that strange aroma, you knew that they were going to die.

Soon afterward, my dad *had* died—my terrible gift had correctly predicted his end. Now it was predicting Jenny's. I knew then that whatever Nora had given Jenny wasn't working. I had to help her now. And there was only one thing I could do.

"I need to stretch my legs," I told Nora, who was sitting beside Jenny once more, mopping her brow.

I returned to the small hallway, which seemed colder than ever. Quickly I rummaged in my bag and pulled out the small mirror I kept there. I held it close to my face, placed the fingers of my left hand against it, and whispered Alice's name.

Only she could save Jenny now. . . .

Nothing happened, so I breathed on the mirror and wrote on it with my forefinger.

Jenny is dying, Alice. Poisoned by a water witch. Please help!

As the steam faded, taking my words with it, the mirror brightened, and for a brief second I thought I saw Alice's face. But with a flicker it was gone, making me think I'd simply imagined it.

Had I made contact? I wondered. Had Alice understood? She could use her magic to travel to the space between worlds, and from there to this house. But she might be occupied with other problems. After all, Malkin Tower was probably under siege. She might need all her magic just to keep the Kobalos mages and warriors at bay.

If the Pendle witches fell, the County would be defenseless. Our soldiers, armed only with guns and blades, would be helpless against the enemy's dark magic.

I turned, intending to go back to see how Jenny was. But before I could do so, Nora emerged into the hallway. She stood facing me, but she didn't meet my gaze.

My heart sank. "What is it?" I asked her. I'd already guessed from her demeanor what she was about to say.

"I'm truly sorry, but Jenny has just passed away. There was nothing I could do to save her," she told me, shaking her head.

I just stared at her, unable to speak, grief choking off the words before I could utter them.

"Would you like to see her?" she asked, looking up for the first time, a slight smile turning up the corners of her mouth—probably just sympathy, I thought, frowning.

"It'd be best to see her now, while she's still warm," Nora continued, "so that your final memory of her will be a good one. The cooling of the blood and flesh brings about terrible changes. Death can be very ugly."

I wasn't really taking in what Nora was saying—I was in shock—though her words seemed a little insensitive. I meekly followed her to the room where Jenny lay.

I knelt down beside the bed and peered closely at her, tears welling. She wasn't breathing, but when I took her hand, it felt warm. She looked very peaceful, almost as if she was sleeping, but she didn't move. I quickly checked for a pulse—first on her wrist and then at her neck, but could find nothing.

Jenny was dead.

I was vaguely aware that Nora was standing directly behind me. I felt something brush against my shoulder, but I hardly registered it because my focus was entirely upon Jenny. My chest was heaving with emotion.

When I realized that Nora was easing the Starblade out of its scabbard, it was almost too late.

I came to my feet and saw that she had the sword grasped in her right hand.

Out of the corner of my eye I saw something shimmering by the door. It was vaguely human in shape, but more bulky, like one of the Kobalos. Something was starting to materialize there.

I lurched forward and put my hand over Nora's, my fingertips on the blade, suddenly realizing the truth.

Nora was a tulpa. She was here either to kill me or get the blade away from me so that my protection against dark magic would be gone.

I glanced back toward the doorway. The shimmering had ceased, but I had no doubt now that if the tulpa managed to keep the blade away from me for more than a few seconds, then a Kobalos mage would appear and use dark magic against me.

I struggled to tear the Starblade out of Nora's grasp. She was incredibly strong, but I was desperate, and I managed to get hold of it again. I stepped back and raised it, ready to deliver a mortal blow.

But all at once, I hesitated. This woman looked exactly

like the Nora I remembered. How could I kill her in cold blood?

But she *wasn't* a woman, I told myself firmly. She was a tulpa, and no doubt she'd let Jenny die so that I would kneel at the bedside, giving her the opportunity to seize the blade.

Suddenly the thing that looked like Nora gave a shrill scream and covered her face with her hands—in fear that I was about to strike her with my sword, I thought.

But I was wrong.

"What have I done? What have I done?" she screamed, lowering her hands and gazing at me with terrified eyes. "I've killed my mistress. Why did I do that?"

She ran out of the room, and I followed her down the corridor and into another bedroom. The housekeeper was lying on the bed there, eyes bulging, the whites red with burst veins. She'd been strangled.

"Poor Mrs. Hesketh!" the tulpa wailed. "She was a harsh mistress, but she always treated me fairly. Why would I do that to her?"

"You did it because you were acting under the control of another," I said softly. "You aren't Nora. You probably killed Nora before taking her place. You're a tulpa."

The transformation began immediately. This disintegration was even faster than that of the tulpa that had believed itself to be Bill Arkwright. This female form had been rotund; now the belly swelled grotesquely, then sagged low, forming an apron, before bursting with a sickening squelch. The mouth began to ooze slime, and the teeth fell out to plop onto the bedroom carpet.

I'd seen enough. There was nothing I could do for the murdered Mrs. Hesketh. Others would have to deal with it. I just had to get away—though I couldn't leave Jenny's body here. I would take it with me and bury her elsewhere.

I went back into the little bedroom and realized that there was one last thing I needed to do for her. I had to check that her soul was not lingering by her body, unable to leave. I certainly didn't want her joining the other ghosts that haunted Chingle Hall.

"Jenny! Jenny! Are you there?" I called softly.

I repeated the question two more times, just to be sure. Her ghost didn't appear, and so, satisfied, I prepared to leave.

I decided that I'd only take my own bag and staff with me. I opened Jenny's bag and stared at the contents, my mind numb with grief, and transferred a few of the items into my bag: the small sacks containing salt and iron, and her personal possessions, including her notebook. Her mother and father were dead, and she hadn't been close to her foster parents. Nevertheless, I resolved to return her things to them one day.

I took the sheet off the bed and spread it out on the floor. Then I lifted up Jenny's body and gently placed her on it. I kissed her on the forehead, then wrapped her in the sheet, knotting the ends as best I could.

I let myself out of the tradesmen's entrance and, carrying Jenny's body over my shoulder and holding my bag and staff in my left hand, headed east along the ley line that would take me most of the way to Malkin Tower.

I hadn't gone more than a hundred yards when I came upon the body of Blood. She'd suffered severe wounds—no doubt the tulpa's work. She was the last of Bill Arkwright's dogs, but there was nothing I could do but leave her there and move on. I was already filled with grief for the poor dead girl I was carrying. There would be other horrors waiting out there, I thought. The real Nora would have died in a similar fashion to the dog.

As I walked, I'd been wondering what to do with Jenny's body. I remembered that churches were frequently found on ley lines, and I knew that one, St. Wilfred's, lay directly ahead of me. I'd never visited it, so I would be gambling on the priest being prepared to allow a spook's apprentice to be buried next to his churchyard. It was the best I could hope for. Some priests considered spooks to be no better than witches or dark mages.

The priest's name was Father Greenalgh, and he proved to be a decent man.

"I'm sorry that I can't allow her to be buried in holy ground—if I did that, my bishop would only have her disinterred. But there's a nice spot just east of the churchyard," he told me.

"Thank you, Father. That's all that I ask," I said.

The sun was rising as we walked up to a hillock shaded by a large yew tree. Father Greenalgh was carrying two spades, and to my surprise he helped me to dig Jenny's grave.

Then he said some prayers while I bowed my head and tried to hold back my tears.

"Would *you* like to say a few words?" he asked.

I nodded and gathered my thoughts. When I spoke, my voice wobbled with emotion. "I chose well in making Jenny my first apprentice. She was a good, brave, and talented girl and would have become a great spook. It's terrible that she was taken from us before she reached her full potential. I'll miss her. . . ."

I had intended to say more, but my voice grew choked with grief.

Father Greenalgh patted me on the shoulder, and we lowered Jenny into the grave and filled it in together.

"Thank you again for your help and consideration," I said to him. "I haven't much money with me, but next time I pass this way I'll make a donation to the church and pay for a stone to mark Jenny's grave."

The priest nodded. "Where are you going now?" he asked.

"Pendle," I answered. "I've business there."

"Well, before you make that journey, come back to the presbytery for some breakfast."

"Thanks again, Father, but my business is urgent, and I need to press on. But I'd just like a few moments alone to pray by the graveside."

"Of course."

Father Greenalgh collected the two spades and set off back toward the church. I waited until he was out of earshot, then said what needed to be said.

"Jenny! Jenny! Are you there?" I called softly.

There wasn't even the faintest breeze, and the birds had fallen silent. I listened carefully.

I uttered the words three times, but there was no reply, and that was good. In the case of a violent death, ghosts sometimes stayed at the scene, which I'd already checked, but most lingered by their graveside. However, spooks knew all about ghosts and would certainly not want to become one. After death they would go to the light, and

I was sure that was what Jenny had done.

She was no longer here.

I picked up my bag and staff, squinted into the sun, and with a heavy heart began to walk east, following the ley line toward Pendle.

As I walked, Jenny filled my thoughts. I would never see her again. How I wished she was walking beside me now, giving me cheek!

It was terrible to lose an apprentice, but I knew that more than a third of the boys my master trained had died violent deaths while fighting the dark.

I had to get used to it.

It would happen again.

Grimalkin

20
Lukrasta's Plan

The cavern shimmered before my gaze. It was good to be able to see it. After being caught in the sun, I'd feared that I would be permanently blind. Warm air swirled sluggishly, stirred by heat that radiated like the hot breath of a giant from the mouth of the glowing forge.

Entranced, I watched the god Hephaestus crouch over an anvil, his shadow monstrous against the wall of rock behind him. Sweat glistened on the knotted muscles of his naked upper body, and his bulbous eyes were fixed in intense concentration. He was one of our allies and was now working at Pan's behest.

Three enormous bellows worked in sequence, pumping air deep into the coals to make them glow first red, then white. Whether they worked by magic, or whether unseen hands squeezed them, I could not tell.

Huge hammers rested against the wall, but the one

Hephaestus held was relatively small, his blows rapid and delicate. He was working a ball of silver alloy, shaping the first of the hands that would replace those cut from Lukrasta by his Kobalos torturers.

"This is astonishing," I whispered to Thorne. "I have skills of my own, and as you know, child, I have always forged my own weapons. But my expertise is nothing compared to what we are witnessing now."

"It's not like you to put yourself down, Grimalkin," she replied. "He has great skill, certainly, but so have you. It is true that he forged the hero swords that were used to slay the Fiend, but you crafted the Starblade. Isn't that an even more formidable weapon?"

"Do you think so?" I asked with a smile. "Only time will tell the truth of that."

"Is the pain lessening?" she asked, staring into my eyes, her own full of concern.

"It is healing, child. The pain is something that I must deal with."

My face had indeed been damaged. When the sun seared into it, my vision had darkened—though I'd already visualized the location of the third Shaiksa and was able to slay him before fleeing those deadly rays.

On my return to the dark, my face had been covered in huge weeping blisters and I had been blind, but Pan had brought me a healer, one of the few Old Gods who are our allies. His name was Asclepius, and he carried a rod about which a snake was coiled. He was tall, thin, and gaunt, with a shock of white hair, and looked more like a pale ghost than a powerful living entity.

He had given me a choice: "There are two options," he'd said. "Which one do you prefer—slow, painless healing, or that which is rapid and agonizing?"

"The latter," I told him.

Asclepius spoke no more, but simply touched my eyes and laid cool hands upon my cheeks. Finally he tapped me three times upon the forehead with the rod, and I heard the snake hiss.

Then the agony began.

Only now was the pain starting to fade, but my face had healed without scars and my sight was as good as ever. Ascelpius had also tended Lukrasta, but that task had proved to be far from easy. He had hoped to regenerate his severed hands, but that was beyond him.

However, with the help of Hephaestus, the mage would soon have silver hands that promised to be even better than the originals. Then he would be forced to return to Earth; there is a limit to the length of time a living human, even if they have the powers of a witch or a mage, can remain in the dark.

Where would he go? I wondered. Back to his tower in Cymru, where he had spent time with Alice?

Pan was sitting on the roots of our tree home, a single raven perched on the branch above his head. No doubt it was a watcher who served him. It looked more alert than he did. His eyes were closed, but he gestured that Lukrasta should speak.

Thorne and I stood aside as the mage outlined his plan. He wore a hooded gown, and those who didn't know he was a mage might have taken him for a spook. As he spoke, he gestured with his new hands. They were a wonder to behold—the fingers flexed as if formed of supple and sensitive skin, flesh and bone rather than silver alloy.

"We need to strike directly at their god, Talkus," he said. "Remove him, and the war against the Kobalos will be almost won. He is their motivation as well as the source of their newly powerful mage magic."

"What do you propose?" Pan asked, opening one eye, his voice full of weariness. He was still very weak; he was panting away like a dog on a hot afternoon and seemed utterly exhausted. I felt sure that, whatever Lukrasta proposed, Pan would agree to it.

By contrast, the mage now appeared strong and full of energy. He had fully recovered from his terrible ordeal as a prisoner of the Kobalos. His thick hair shone and tumbled out from under his hood onto his shoulders. His lips, partially obscured by his mustache, were suffused with blood. I had rescued an emaciated, broken man, but now he appeared youthful, his whole body strong and vigorous. It was a tremendous change in so short a time—no doubt brought about by the healing abilities of Ascelpius, combined with the power of his own magic.

"I intend to lure Talkus to my tower in Cymru. Using the store of magic that I have accumulated there, I can move the tower through time. I will bind him, then transport him into an epoch in which he is far from comfortable and abandon him there. But in order to achieve that, I will need Alice to join her magic with mine once more."

"Is Alice to have no say in this?" I demanded.

"Alice will see the need for our renewed alliance," Lukrasta said, glaring at me. "Besides, we have been very close friends, and I am sure she will want to continue the relationship."

"She is with Tom Ward now," I remarked coldly. "I think you might be misjudging the situation."

Pan had opened both eyes now; he glanced at me and then at Lukrasta. "What you propose could lead to victory, so it is well worth attempting. I will command Alice to do as you ask," he told him.

On the face of it, Alice and Lukrasta should indeed unite and attempt to destroy Talkus. But there was something wrong here, I thought . . . something I couldn't quite put my finger on. I had grave misgivings.

"You have an important part to play in luring Talkus to my tower, Grimalkin," Lukrasta said, smiling at me in a supercilious way.

"Then tell me what it is," I said coldly, itching to draw my blades and cut the smirk from his face.

"There is a castle in Polyznia where I believe you spent some time. Tom Ward's apprentice explored an attic high in a turret there and found a portal that leads to Talkus's lair. I want you to enter this attic and provoke the god into pursuing you, leading him to my tower, where everything will be prepared to receive him."

"That portal is guarded by a powerful demon. Tom's apprentice, Jenny, barely escaped with her life," I pointed out.

"That will surely prove to be of little hindrance to you, Grimalkin. Once the demon erupts from the portal, slip past him and enter his domain. They say you like a challenge—one that tests your mettle. What more could you want than to grab a god by his tail?"

"What makes you think that he will pursue me? Why should he do that?" I asked Lukrasta.

"You will have taken from him something he values greatly—the greater part of his soul!" he replied.

"And how may I seize his soul?"

"Part of his soul lies within his body. *That* you cannot touch. But the bulk of it is still contained within a fleshy pouch connected to him by a tube—somewhat like a child within a mother's womb, drawing nutrition into its body through the umbilical cord. Once Talkus has absorbed the whole of his soul stuff from that container, he will be at full strength. But until then he is vulnerable. Seize the pouch, and he must follow. Lure him to my tower, and I will do the rest."

I turned to Pan with a frown. "If he follows me, then he must surely pass through your domain. Will you allow that?" I asked him.

"He will follow you to Lukrasta's tower, but will take a different route than you," Pan stated flatly. "He will not attempt to pass through here."

I nodded, realizing that it was useless to protest. I could see no flaw in the plan: if I could lure the god to Lukrasta's tower and he did as the mage had planned, we would have won. Deprived of their new god, the power of the Kobalos and their mages would surely wane.

So I said nothing, and within the hour Lukrasta had left the dark and gone to meet Alice. Then they would head directly for his tower in Cymru.

"I don't like it, Grimalkin," Thorne said, once we were alone. "It's easy for him to talk, but you will be the one in danger. I wish I could help you, but that shamanistic skill is difficult—I've still some way to go."

"Keep persevering. Eventually you will succeed. But I must attempt this task alone, child. If I could think of a better way, I'd put it forward. We'll just have to make the best of things."

Tom Ward

21
Within the Devil's Triangle

I strode north along the western flank of Pendle. My intention was to pass the village of Downham—the route my master had always preferred.

By now my sadness at Jenny's death had turned to rage. It was so unfair. Why had it happened? I kept wondering what I could have done differently. With the growing anger came guilt to weigh me down. *I should have given her injury priority,* I thought bitterly. I knew of at least two healers who worked north of Caster. I should have taken her there immediately.

But no—in my eagerness to press on toward Malkin Tower and Alice, I had brought about Jenny's death. I would make my enemies pay for that mistake. I still had the Starblade. If I could find the Kobalos god, Talkus, and get close to him, I could use the sword to slay him. Once I was reunited with Alice, that would be my chief objective. There had to be a way to accomplish this . . . and I would find it.

At first Pendle was hard to make out, but then the moon rose in the east, and suddenly, as I finally approached the outskirts of the village, the hill was before me, rearing up like a huge, threatening beast.

My master, John Gregory, had once commented that its shape reminded some people of a beached whale—although, since I had never seen a beached whale, that was of little help to me. Another comparison was to an upturned boat. But if you had to come up with a single word to describe Pendle, it was "menacing."

It was no coincidence that the majority of the County witch clans had made their home close by. Some parts of the Earth had their own built-in power and were particularly suited to the use of dark magic; Pendle was certainly one of these.

Malkin Tower stood in a clearing in a wood east of the hill. From its battlements, rising high above the trees that surrounded it, you could look down on the wood and see Pendle Hill beyond it. But the majority of the tower's interior lay below ground. There were dungeons where the Malkins used to torture their enemies. John Gregory had once worked his way through the cells one by one, sending the dead to the light.

However, I had no intention of going directly through the village of Downham. There might be Kobalos there—or their spies. It was best that nobody knew I was here. Once Downham had been clear of witches. A strong priest called Father Stocks had kept the area safe, but he was dead now, and things might have changed for the worse.

The clans were always at each other's throats. *Why should things change?* I thought. It wasn't too far-fetched to suppose that some might even be on the side of the Kobalos. There were witches who were so greedy for dark magic that they'd do anything to get it, and the Kobalos mages certainly had plenty to offer.

I knew that the farther south I traveled down that eastern flank of the hill, the more dangerous things would get. Witches generally stayed farther south, in what's sometimes called the Devil's Triangle. Three main villages lay within the triangle: Bareleigh, Roughlee, and Goldshaw Booth. The last of these had already been attacked and burned—there would definitely be Kobalos there; maybe they'd have some witch allies too.

After about half an hour, I glanced east, to where the moon illuminated the treetops of a small wood in a valley. This was Witch Dell—one of the most dangerous places in the whole district, the home of many dead witches.

Most were weak and could only crawl about catching mice and eating slugs and worms. But there were also a couple of really strong ones who might be out hunting tonight. I just hoped they'd choose Kobalos warriors rather than me for their prey—I didn't want anything slowing me down. Nevertheless, if anything from the dark got in my way, I was more than ready for it.

At last I spotted my destination—the stark outline of Malkin Tower rising out of the clearing at the heart of Crow Wood. The sight of it brought back so many memories, most of them bad. I remembered Agnes Sowerbutts, Alice's aunt, who'd been slain by our enemies close to that tower. I'd last met her in Witch Dell; she was now one of the dead witches there. Was she still in the dell? I wondered. Witches didn't last forever in Witch Dell; they slowly disintegrated, bit by bit.

As I approached the wood, I smelled smoke and saw distant campfires at its periphery. It could be witches, I thought, maybe even those who were enemies of the Kobalos. But Alice had told me that our allies were already inside the tower. It was too risky to approach them, so I headed away from the fires, taking a longer route.

I soon found myself in an abandoned churchyard choked with bushes and saplings. I knew that there was a way in that avoided the densest part of the thicket. The place hadn't changed much since my last visit. Tombstones stood at crazy angles, most of them hidden by the wild, unchecked growth, and I glimpsed the ruin of the church through the trees—just two low walls were still standing.

I approached the small building that lay directly ahead of me. A sycamore tree had sprouted up through the roof, bringing most of it down. Four years ago, when I'd first visited this place, it had been a young tree, hardly more than a sapling. Now it rose high above the walls. This ruin was a sepulchre built long ago for a rich family. Some of their bones still lay there. I'd have to climb onto one of the shelves and squeeze down over the ledge into the tunnel.

Suddenly I remembered what poor Jenny had said. I wondered if the tunnel was still a secret. Or were my enemies waiting to ambush me there?

Before entering the sepulchre, I took the lantern from my bag and lit it, adjusting the shutters so that it cast its light upon the ground. Then I rummaged around for the special key that John Gregory's locksmith brother had made and placed it in my left breeches pocket.

However, I found that, as usual, this first door wasn't locked. I walked in, moving the shutters on the lantern so that the chamber of bones was partly illuminated. There was a stench of rot and decay here. Most of the stone shelves contained complete skeletons, but on one, the bones had been dislodged. I eased first my bag, then my staff, through the gap and let them go. It wasn't a long drop. The first section of tunnel was low.

It was a tight squeeze for me to fit through, but even so I didn't risk removing the Starblade. Anything could lurk down there in the darkness; the moment when I was squeezing through into the tunnel would be the most dangerous of all. Blades or teeth could be lying in wait for me—though the Starblade would keep me safe from Kobalos dark magic.

I crawled onto the cold shelf and, leaving the lantern behind me, dropped into the tunnel headfirst, tensed for a sudden attack. Moments later I was kneeling at the bottom, trying to control my rapid breathing and looking up at the oblong of yellow light from above. The ceiling was low; there wasn't enough room for me to stand.

I reached up through the gap and eased the lantern down into the tunnel, holding it so that I could see ahead. At the moment there seemed to be no danger. Perhaps the tunnel was still a secret. I just had to hope so.

Grasping my staff and lantern in my left hand and my bag in my right, I crawled forward. I'd never liked this first section of the secret passageway. There were no supports holding up the roof; just a tremendous weight of earth that might collapse at any moment to trap and suffocate anyone below.

At last the tunnel emerged into an earthen chamber, where the ceiling was high enough for me to stand. The next section of tunnel was just as I remembered: tall enough for me to walk, and supported by stout wooden props. It was very narrow, but soon it widened out into an oval cave with a small stagnant lake at its center.

This pool had once been home to a wight, a creature created by witches by binding the soul of a drowned sailor to his bloated body. It had guarded the tunnel, but had been slain by a lamia witch. Now, it was safe to pass.

The path skirted the lake to the left; it was muddy and slippery, so I walked carefully. Suddenly, close to me, the water brightened, and I saw Alice's face looking up at me. She was frowning as she mouthed a message.

"You're in danger, Tom. Please take care. Help's on its way."

Then she vanished, and I was left staring down into the stagnant pool. What if there were skelts down there—or even water witches? I wondered. It was certainly possible. I knew that it was extremely deep and might well contain a threat.

I headed away from the water, on into the narrow tunnel, holding the lantern high in my right hand, my bag and staff in my left. I hadn't taken more than a couple of dozen paces when I saw something moving directly ahead of me.

At first glance the figures appeared to be human rather than Kobalos; they were coming toward me, and I soon identified them.

They were incredibly thin, with spindly arms and legs. Their mouths dripped with saliva and hung open to reveal long, needlelike teeth. . . .

22

A Mound of Bodies

Although I'd never seen one of the zanti, I'd read Grimalkin's notes on the creatures.

They were one of the entities she'd grown and studied from samples taken from the tree home of the haizda mage I'd slain, experimenting to determine their strengths and weaknesses. They were one of many different battle entities created by Kobalos mages to attack humans.

Their foreheads and cheeks were covered with black scales, and the small eyes were wide set. Those scales were tough. The zanti were much smaller than the varteki, but they were also designed for battle, and used for close combat.

As they advanced, the creatures cocked their heads from side to side, making small jerky movements like birds. There seemed to be no more than seven or eight of them, but others might well be lurking in the shadows. The ones I could see were armed with long blades and short axes—though the tunnel was narrow, with room for only one of them to attack at a time. This was something that tipped the odds in my favor.

I set my lantern, bag, and staff down on the ground. Then I strode forward, drawing the Starblade from its scabbard.

I lunged at the foremost creature; it was fast, and its ax parried my blade. I couldn't see much, but I struck again, slicing away its thin left arm close to the shoulder. It screamed and retreated, another stepping forward to take its place.

I quickly despatched the second, swinging hard from left to right, and had the satisfaction of feeling the blade bite deep. A third came for me, and then a fourth, but I dealt out death to each creature that opposed me.

Suddenly, acting as one, the remaining zanti turned and fled.

Despite their retreat, I still felt uneasy. These creatures had surely given up too easily. No doubt this had been a patrol, now heading back to summon reinforcements; they would probably choose a better place to fight—one where they could bring their weight of numbers to bear.

Alice had said that help was on its way, though. Behind

me, beyond the entrance to the tunnel and the graveyard, my enemies lay in wait. Surely no aid would be coming from out there. Where else could it be waiting but in the tower above? Instinct told me to keep going.

It was then that I sensed a movement at my back. I turned and lifted the lantern, and saw the unmistakable outline of another entity. I'd been right to be mistrustful of the pool; danger had indeed been lurking in its depths. A skelt was scuttling toward me on its many legs; others were surging along the tunnel behind it, their bone tubes extended threateningly.

They had waited for me to move on before emerging, thus cutting off my escape route. I was trapped; there was now danger ahead and behind.

I sheathed the Starblade, snatched up my staff, bag, and lantern and ran forward along the tunnel. Ahead of me, the door that led up into the tower now stood open. It was almost like an invitation. No doubt the zanti were waiting on the other side.

I went through cautiously and held up the lantern to illuminate the darkness. I could see the passage ahead and the cells on either side where the Malkins used to keep their prisoners. Were there zanti lurking inside, ready to ambush me?

I closed the door behind me and, taking the key from

my breeches pocket, pushed it into the lock. I had to jiggle it about before it would turn, but that key rarely let me down. The door was now locked, and I felt confident that it was stout enough to keep the skelts at bay. That was one threat dealt with, but how many zanti lay ahead of me?

I moved cautiously down the passageway, checking the cells one by one. At the first two I paused to ready my staff and glanced left, then right. They were empty but for the bones of those who'd died in captivity, so I moved forward to the next, which was also empty.

But the fourth . . .

The first thing that warned me was the stench of blood. Then I peered in and saw a mound of bodies. They were dead witches, their sightless eyes wide open, their faces a rictus of pain and terror. They were covered in blood, which had formed a red moat around them. I realized that they had died very recently. The blood was still dripping from them.

Closer inspection told me that the bodies belonged to more than one of the Pendle clans. Two of the clans had no obvious distinguishing marks: there was no way to judge from her dress or her weapon whether a witch was a Malkin or a Deane. But the Mouldheels always went barefoot, and I noticed that some of the dead witches were not wearing pointy shoes. Nor had these been lost in combat—I could see the hard calluses on the yellow soles.

Was this the help that had been on its way? I wondered. Had the zanti massacred these witches? If so, how many of the creatures awaited me in the tower?

It was then that an unbearable thought slipped into my head.

What if Alice had been slain too? What if her corpse formed part of this mound of the dead?

Then I caught sight of something so terrible that I swayed and almost fell. One of the legs sticking out from the pile of corpses was wearing a pointy shoe I recognized.

It looked like Alice's.

23

The Refuge of the Witches

Frantically I began to pull the dead off the heap, sliding their bodies to the ground, working my way down toward that foot in its pointy shoe.

When I reached it, I let out a sigh of relief, my whole body trembling. The shoe was very similar to the ones Alice wore, but it wasn't hers.

I continued to slide witches off the pile, carefully checking each dead face, looking for Alice but desperately hoping that I wouldn't find her.

At last the grim work was done and I paused for a moment, allowing my breathing to return to normal.

I stared at the corpses that were now scattered across the cell and felt a tear trickle down my cheek; I shivered with cold and emotion. At last I took a deep breath and brought my body back under control, then picked up my staff, bag, and lantern and left the cell. Cautiously I glanced into each of the remaining cells. Apart from a few skeletons and the odd bone, all were empty.

I went on and entered the huge circular chamber at the center of the cellar. I could hear the sound of dripping water—the ancient tower was surrounded by a leaking moat, and this room lay deep underground. But I was alert for other sounds . . . anything that might indicate the presence of zanti.

The chamber was mostly as I remembered it. Five pillars hung with chains and manacles supported the high ceiling. Two things were missing, though: the wooden table with its instruments of torture, and the metal brazier where the witches heated their knives, tongs, and pincers.

Maybe the Malkins had stopped torturing their enemies . . . but I dismissed the thought immediately. It was unlikely that they had changed. Surely the bitter conflict between the clans had continued. I thought back to the mound of corpses, formed from witches from all three clans. This surely meant that Alice had succeeded in forging some sort of alliance between them so that they had united against our common enemy. Though in this case, they had not prevailed.

I looked at the stone steps that circled the walls of the tower; they led to the trapdoor that gave access to its upper reaches. This door stood open now. Had the zanti climbed through it, or were they still on this level? There were other passageways and other cells here; they could be lurking anywhere.

Relying on my instincts, as my master had taught me, I decided to climb into the higher levels of the tower. Surely Alice had to be somewhere up there. At the trap-door, I peered up, but it was pitch black. Anything could be lurking there. I put down my staff and bag and lifted the lantern, holding it to the opening until I saw the damp curve of the wall beyond.

Nothing was moving. All I could hear was dripping water. I poked my head and shoulders through and then held the lantern high. The steps spiraled on upward, but they were deserted. Apart from the sound of dripping, there was silence.

Setting my lantern down on the flagged floor beyond the door, I climbed through. Then, all at once, I heard a noise from above—a metallic clang.

I froze where I was and waited, but the sound wasn't repeated. I gazed at the narrow spiraling steps that disappeared into the darkness far above. They looked very slippery. The green slime that covered the walls had extended to the stairs; no doubt more and more water was seeping through the stones from the moat above.

The higher I got, the more dangerous it would become. A slip might well be fatal.

I remembered that Jenny hadn't been too happy with heights. These slippery steps would have made her nervous—though she'd been brave; she would have climbed them anyway. It would have been so good to have her alongside me now. Two heads were always better than one when assessing danger. I missed her.

I picked up my things and climbed slowly, keeping my right shoulder hard against the wall and trying not to look down into the stairwell. Cells lined the staircase, so I needed to be watchful. The zanti had to be somewhere.

It was cold, and my breath steamed in the air ahead of me. Approaching the first cell, I held up the lantern to peer inside. It was empty, and so was the next. At last I reached the cell I remembered so well. My brother Jack and his wife and child had been held captive here, brought to Pendle by the witches who had raided their farm. This cell was empty too.

I paused and glanced down the stairwell to my left. The floor was already a long way below.

I continued to climb, my footsteps echoing off the stones. I was nearing the top now. There wasn't much farther to go. What would I find when I got there? I wondered. I wanted Alice to be waiting for me, but I didn't hold out much hope of that. My heart was racing with dread. I couldn't bear the thought of losing her again. The help she'd promised hadn't arrived, and then I'd found all those dead witches. If all was well, Alice would surely have known that I was on my way; she would have come down the steps to greet me. The fact that she hadn't didn't bode well.

I wondered what could have stopped someone with such powerful magic at her disposal. Maybe it had been an overwhelming force—hordes of zanti or Kobalos warriors. Or it might have been Balkai, the most powerful mage of the triumvirate, who had no doubt created the dangerous tulpas I'd encountered, but had yet to show his face.

Only one possibility was worse: the direct intervention of Talkus.

The trapdoor at the top of the steps was open; it was strange that it wasn't locked and guarded, I reflected. I climbed through into the storeroom, which was full of provisions—sacks of potatoes, carrots, rutabagas, and turnips—and then headed into the large room beyond, the place where the Malkins lived and worked at their spells. I stood there for a moment, looking around. The chamber was full of witches.

There were at least two hundred Pendle witches

gathered there, though apart from the drone of snores, the room was quiet. Most of them were sleeping. There was a smell of sweat and cooking, and the place was cluttered with sacks and mattresses and dirty plates.

In the far corner, thirteen witches sat cross-legged in a circle on the floor. They weren't speaking, but their faces were fixed in concentration. One or two of them I recognized. In the air above them, something was shimmering. I realized that this was the Malkin coven creating some form of magical spell.

Heads were starting to turn toward me now. No doubt the trapdoor hadn't been guarded because they thought there were witches on watch below. They didn't yet realize that they'd all been slain.

Two witches were standing to one side, and they both approached me immediately. The first I didn't recognize: she was tall and fierce, and scowled at me as if we were deadly enemies. At her belt she carried seven long blades, and a thin wooden tube hung from a chain around her neck. She reminded me a little of Grimalkin. Was this the new assassin of the Malkin clan? I wondered.

However, I knew the other witch, who was barefooted. It was Mab, the young leader of the Mouldheels. She had long pale hair and green eyes and was quite pleasing to look at—though I knew that she wasn't to be trusted.

She was a blood witch, and sometimes the stink of her breath was worse than a dog's.

She smiled at me. "Good to see you, Tom. My, how handsome you've grown! Where's Beth, that ugly sister of mine? Glad she found you and brought you up here safely," she said, looking over my shoulder as if expecting to see her sister at any moment.

There was no easy way to break the news to her. Her other sister had died fighting on our side at the Battle of the Wardstone. Now the second twin was dead.

"I'm sorry, Mab, but I have some bad news. Your sister is dead. She and all the other witches that were sent to help me were killed by the zanti before I arrived. Their bodies are in the cells below."

Mab let out a terrible wail and covered her face with her hands. The other witch clasped her left hand around the hilt of one of her long daggers; she looked as if she wanted to cut my heart out.

"Where's Alice?" I asked her, ignoring her hostile expression.

"Someone came to claim her," the witch replied, a malicious smile on her face. "She had more important things to do than hang around waiting for you. She went off with the mage Lukrasta."

24
Makrilda, the Witch Assassin

I just stared at her, trying to make sense of what she was saying. How could Alice have gone off with Lukrasta when he was dead?

Then, all at once, I was assailed with doubt. *Was* he dead? That was what Alice had told me, but could she have been lying? The fact that I'd been rushing to Alice's side had cost Jenny her life. I couldn't bear the thought that she had betrayed me after all.

No, I reflected, it was more likely that the witch before me lied.

"Is that the truth?" I asked, directing my anger at her.

"Be careful, spook. It is dangerous to call me a liar," she hissed. "I am Makrilda, the assassin of the Malkin clan. Your thumbs would make a good addition to my collection of bones. So don't give me an excuse to cut them off!"

I was filled with an anger so extreme that I lost control of myself. Instead of taking a deep breath and containing my wrath, I stepped forward and struck her hard on the right shoulder with my open palm. She staggered backward but quickly regained her balance.

A moment later she was holding a blade in each hand.

Makrilda attacked. She was fast. . . .

But I was faster.

As she charged toward me, I struck each of her wrists with the base of my staff and knocked the blades out of her grasp. Then I thrust out my staff, positioning the tip behind her left ankle, using a trick I'd learned from Bill Arkwright.

When our shoulders made contact, she went sprawling backward. I stood looking down at her. I knew I could never have managed to down Grimalkin so easily.

But it wasn't over yet. She came back up onto her knees, already reaching for two more blades.

All at once Mab came between us. "Stupid, this is!" she cried. "We are supposed to be allies."

I nodded and lowered my staff, ashamed. I shouldn't have reacted like that, but too many bad things had happened recently. I wasn't myself.

"Look, I didn't intend to imply that you're a liar," I said to the witch assassin as she got to her feet. "I am sorry if I offended you. It's just that I find what you say very hard to believe." I was trying to stay calm. "I believed Lukrasta to be dead."

"Very much alive, he is, Tom," Mab said, rubbing her tear-streaked face with the back of her hand. "He has hands made out of silver, but they're wick with life and move just like flesh, skin, and bone. He spent a long time talking to Alice, and then they both vanished without a word to anyone. No doubt they had more important things to do than stay around to help us. My sister died trying to save you—it was Alice who asked her to lead those witches on a rescue mission. And then Alice didn't even stay to find out if you were all right!"

Alice had told me that the Kobalos had chopped off Lukrasta's hands, so the story of the silver hands supported Makrilda's claim. He'd probably replaced them using his powerful magic. A whole mix of feelings surged through me; the first one was jealousy.

Alice had gone off with Lukrasta again. However, I told myself, she was an earth witch and served Pan. If the god had insisted, she might have had no choice.

The second feeling was fear.

A disturbing thought drifted into my mind. I remembered the two tulpas I'd encountered. Each time I'd been completely taken in. What if Lukrasta was a tulpa too?

Then there was another disturbing possibility. The Kobalos mages were skilled at creating illusions and deceit. What if Balkai had taken on the shape of the human mage? After all, in northern Polyznia, the Kobalos mage Lenklewth had once taken on Lukrasta's shape. The illusion had been good enough to fool me and Grimalkin. It seemed that Alice might well now be in the clutches of our enemies.

An uneasy truce now existed between Makrilda and me. She kept giving me resentful glances, and I knew that one day she would seek revenge for what I had done. Not all the witches had been asleep, and the seated coven had also witnessed our fight. Makrilda had been bested by a spook, and her pride would be hurt. She could only regain face by killing me.

However, I had more important things to worry about now.

The Malkin coven had decided that attack was the best form of defense. Instead of seeking out and repulsing the zanti that had invaded the lower levels of the tower, they sealed and locked the lower trapdoor to prevent the zanti from reaching the section that lay aboveground. Now they were planning to attack their enemies outside the walls, and they would start by taking back what was left of Goldshaw Booth, the Malkin village.

* * *

We made our way to the huge main door of the tower, and I heard the clang and clank of chains as the drawbridge mechanism was deployed. It was slowly lowered across the moat; then bolts were slammed back, freeing the door.

Makrilda led the charge, and the Malkins surged out across to the far bank—fierce, black-gowned women clutching blades, some with knives tied to long poles. They were followed by Mab and the Mouldheels, then a few Deanes, and then me. I was prepared to fight, but I was wary. I sensed a hint of desperation in this attack.

I had come to Malkin Tower not only to be with Alice but to help to defend it against the Kobalos. It would have been hard for the Kobalos to breach its defenses. Was this attack the best option? I wondered. Who knew what forces would oppose us? I wasn't prepared to throw my life away on some foolish doomed assault—although there was no point in staying trapped inside the tower. The Malkins had left a small force to defend it, but there were probably still zanti lurking below; if this attack failed, the zanti would eventually break through the door.

Malkin Tower was located just within the Devil's Triangle; at its northern apex lay the village of Bareleigh, home of the Mouldheels; to the southeast was Roughlee, home of the Deanes. We were now heading southwest toward Goldshaw Booth, which formed the third point of that dark triangle, and we soon left the trees of Crow Wood behind. When I glanced back, I could still see the tower rising above them.

The Malkins had sprinted across the clearing into the trees, brandishing weapons, shrieking and shouting defiance, expecting a battle. But any enemies hiding there had already withdrawn, so we slowed down and trudged across the soggy ground toward Goldshaw Booth. The Malkin force was still being led by Makrilda; meanwhile, I stayed to the rear of the main band of witches.

By now the moon had set, and to the east the sky was already growing lighter. The vast bulk of Pendle Hill obscured most of the heavens to our right. Soon I estimated that we were approaching the village. There was no sign of campfires ahead, but there was smoke in the air; I could taste it in the back of my throat.

In the distance I could hear what sounded like the occasional boom of thunder coming from the direction of Burnley . . . or was it the firing of a big eighteen-pounder gun? There was a barracks in Burnley. Maybe County soldiers were fighting the Kobalos there.

As we approached the village, we saw bodies lying on the ground—so many that we had to pick our way through them. These were Malkin witches who had died defending their village, but I realized that there were an equal number of dead Kobalos warriors, and even more zanti.

The Kobalos mages had sought to end the magical threat posed by the Pendle witches and had gone some way toward achieving that aim. The force of surviving Malkins—those able to fight and wield dark magic—had been vastly reduced, but they still had their coven of thirteen.

Then, ahead of us, I heard shrieks—and the unmistakable sounds of battle. The Malkin vanguard had engaged the enemy.

I started to move forward through the press of witches. When I reached the fighting, I put down my bag and staff and pulled the Starblade from its scabbard—just in time to face the first of the zanti. I started slicing and stabbing, with devastating effect.

Soon I became lost in the moment, cutting and parrying, moving steadily forward, hearing the clash of weapons and the screams of the wounded and dying. I saw Makrilda ahead and to my left, fighting with efficient fury. I doubted whether she was the equal of Grimalkin, but I could not deny that she was forcing the enemy back. In time, who knew what she might achieve?

But first she had to survive this battle.

At first we seemed to be winning, steadily driving the Kobalos and zanti back, but then, very suddenly, things changed.

All at once my limbs felt as heavy as lead and I could barely draw breath. Immediately I knew that dark magic was being used against us. It was like an avalanche rushing down a mountainside, threatening to crush and overturn everything in its path.

I had experienced a similar feeling at the Battle of the Wardstone. So powerful was the magic used against us then that for a while not one member of our force, which included many witches, had been capable of taking a step forward. But seventh sons of seventh sons have a degree of immunity against dark magic. My master, John Gregory, had managed to resist the spell first, and soon he'd been joined by Grimalkin. They'd fought back to back until he was slain. Separated in the press of battle, I hadn't even seen him fall.

The effect was similar now. I felt the blast of dark magic forcing me back. I was in no immediate danger because I was gripping the Starblade, but I glanced about me and saw the strained, twitching faces of the Malkins. Some were attempting to mutter counterspells, but their eyes were bulging, their skin stretched tightly across their cheeks as if they were braving a gale-force wind.

I saw that Makrilda was in serious trouble. A huge warrior, clad in full armor but for the helmet, was driving her back. She was still able to fight, but her blows were lethargic and weak. I knew that, hobbled by Kobalos magic, she would soon fall victim to the whirling sabers.

Then I realized that the Kobalos before her was far more than just a warrior. His face was clean-shaven: he was a mage and, judging by his size, almost certainly a high mage.

Was this Balkai? I wondered. Was he the source of the blast of power that had stalled our advance?

Grimalkin

25
The Portal

I stood beside Thorne and once more combined the power of the cauldron with the power that lay within me. The four paths slowly began to spin. Soon they were whirling by so fast that I could hardly distinguish them. For a while there were many more than four.

This was the hardest thing I had ever attempted with the cauldron. This time I needed access to two places.

At last it was done. Ahead of me, at the end of the path, I could see the towers of the castle in Polyznia; when I turned to gaze in the opposite direction, through the trees, I spotted the dark tower in Cymru.

Then I turned once more and took the path toward Polyznia.

Reaching Earth was easier this time. There was hardly any pain—just a mild discomfort that passed in seconds. I wondered if it might be because I had spent time inuring myself to pain of all kinds. When I was alive, I'd even managed to ignore the constant agony of the silver pin that had held my shattered leg together. Perhaps I had carried that strength across into the dark with me? If so, that training had served me well.

Whatever the cause, the result was good. Previously, the moment when I landed on Earth had been very dangerous in my debilitated state. Now I could appear and immediately strike swiftly at my enemies, whatever the situation.

I reached the edge of the trees and stood gazing at the castle that had once belonged to Prince Stanislaw. He was dead, killed in battle, and it was now in the hands of the Kobalos.

It was dark, a cloudy night with no stars or moon visible. However, the green tinge meant that I could see clearly, every detail more vivid than when I'd gazed upon this scene with living eyes. This castle, I remembered, was hard to defend, and had been used as a hunting lodge; here Prince Stanislaw had entertained his nobles. As the first Kobalos crossed the Shanna River, it had been abandoned.

Few of the enemy were in sight. Half a dozen warriors stood guard before the main entrances. Of course the Kobalos front line was hundreds of miles to the south, and most of their soldiers would be stationed there. They probably assumed that this castle, deep behind their lines, was safe from threat.

Now I would try to implement Lukrasta's plan.

The tallest of the castle's turrets was my objective. That was where the portal to the lair of Talkus was located. I quickly became an orb and soared above the trees toward that turret. Passing through the ancient stones, I found myself at the top of a spiral of stone steps, facing a heavy wooden door. To my surprise, it was open, hanging from its hinges. Someone had forced their way in. I knew that Jenny had locked it after leaving. So who had done this? I wondered.

I returned to my human shape, drew two long blades, then stepped through the doorway and entered a small antechamber containing a table and chairs covered in a thick layer of dust. The portal lay beyond the next door, which had also been forced open. As I entered the larger room, I saw that apart from the two bodies lying in the entrance—no doubt Kobalos soldiers who had blundered in looking for loot—it was exactly as Jenny had described it to me. The bodies were dry and shriveled, the flesh burned to the bone in places. They had been blasted by the targon, the guardian of the portal.

This chamber had once been someone's luxurious

living quarters, but the damp had spoiled it. Water dripped from the ceiling, and the saturated carpets were dark with mold. Four couches surrounded what appeared to be a dark well. This was the portal to the domain of Talkus.

Jenny had described how a wineglass standing on top of the stones around the portal had appeared to fill with red wine, seemingly out of thin air, with not even a ghostly hand visible—though the stench that filled the room told her that it was blood, not wine. The glass had toppled down into the darkness, and she had waited to hear the splash . . . but it had never reached the bottom, and she had realized that this well was a door to the Kobalos dark. Moments later, the room had grown warmer and the terrible tentacled guardian of the portal had risen into view.

There was no warmth here, just a chill damp. Perhaps the guardian would sense me and stir into action, rising up to confront me? I waited, but nothing happened, so I pushed my way between the couches and drew a long dagger. I scratched its point along the top of the stones, making a grating sound that filled the whole chamber and echoed back up from the depths of the portal.

Still there was no response.

I leaned over and peered down into the darkness.

Then I coughed phlegm into my throat and spat a thick globule into the portal. "Here I am!" I cried. "Come and face Grimalkin, if you dare!"

There was a stirring far below, a breath of warmth in my face, then increasing heat; the stones began to steam. The temperature increased rapidly, and something began to rise out of the well toward me. The stones were now hissing and spluttering. Then the creature below took a deep breath, sucking air into its lungs like the huge bellows of Hephaestus's forge.

I retreated a little way, knowing what to expect. A bulging, glowing mass rose above the lip of the portal and hovered in the air above, long tentacles coiling and writhing, glowing eyes glaring at me. The targon stank of rot and decay.

I stepped back again, slowly retreating toward the back of the chamber. The ghost of a Kobalos mage that haunted one of the other towers had told Tom and Jenny that the dark guardian was bound here and could not leave the portal—though its tentacles could surely extend into the farthest corner of this chamber.

"Here I am, you ugly blob of slime!" I taunted. "Here I am!"

I waved my blade at it, and it began to drift toward me, tentacles extended. As soon as it reached me, I sheathed my blade and once again became an orb of light. I soared above it and sped through the narrow gap between its enormous scaly back and the ceiling. Then I dived down into the blackness of the portal, heading for the lair of Talkus.

Tom Ward

26
The Two Towers

I struggled forward, holding my sword at the ready. If the mage slayed the Malkins' assassin, then the witches would quickly lose heart and flee—I was sure of it. This was a critical moment.

It was a battle to reach Makrilda, and I thought I was already too late: she'd fallen to her knees, helpless before the descending sabers of the huge mage. But by sheer force of will, no doubt aided by my natural immunity against dark magic, I stood between the mage and the assassin.

I saw him glance at the Starblade, but then he attacked, sabers whirling. I retreated two steps, then brought the sword down, aiming for his left shoulder. He blocked the blade expertly, but the force of the contact made him stagger backward a step.

Now the mage drew himself up to his full height and

glared at me, his eyes full of arrogance. "I knew that we would meet one day. I also foresaw the outcome—your death!" he boasted. "I am the one born to slay you!"

I stared up into his eyes. "Do they call you Balkai?" I asked, realizing that, all around us, the battle had come to a halt; that all waited to see what would happen next. The mage had already defeated Makrilda. If I also fell to his blades, then he and the Kobalos would have won.

"No, my name is Kordo," he replied. "Balkai is the greatest of all mages, far more powerful in magic and martial skills than I could ever hope to be. Despite that, I am the one who will end your life. That sword will not save you."

I felt a moment of disappointment at the discovery that this was not Balkai. To slay *him* would have been a significant step toward victory over our enemies. But if I could defeat this mage, my victory would turn the tide of battle here.

"What you didn't foresee was your own demise," I told him. "Prophecy is unreliable, and even the greatest of scryers cannot see their own death. You say you saw *my* death? Well, learn this before *you* die! We make the future with every step we take. Nothing is fixed—nothing at all!"

It was what my master, John Gregory, had taught me. It was what I truly believed.

Then I attacked, driving Kordo backward. He fought well, but I soon got through his defenses and the sword bit into his armor high on the left shoulder.

The armor worn by a Kobalos high mage consists of a long coat of layered metal plates. The hem comes well below the knee, and even the throat is well protected—but for some reason these mages often fight without a helmet. Whether this is out of bravado or is designed to encourage an opponent to concentrate on the head while they ready some counterblow, it is impossible to say. But strangely, Kordo's lack of a helmet made me wary of attempting a cut to the head.

Besides, his armor, impressive as it was, could not protect him fully against the Starblade. I'd cut through such armor before. Not only that; when I grew filled with self-belief, the Starblade increased in power. Now I could feel it responding to each flex of my muscles and every movement of my legs and arms, as if it was an extension of my own body.

I truly believed now, and knew deep down, that I had the skill and speed to slay this warrior mage. I'd never felt more determined. I continued to drive him backward, and started to cut away pieces of his armor—a plate low on his left side; another high on his right shoulder, which began to ooze blood.

I concentrated hard, careful not to make a mistake, for I wore no armor. One successful strike from those dual sabers would maim or even kill me.

However, if the tide started to turn against me, I had one final card to play—a gift that had come to my rescue on several occasions in the past. I had the ability to slow or even halt time. It was a difficult gift to use, and my skill had waned. I knew that my gifts were not stable; they could not always be commanded with ease.

So I fought on, relying on my combat skills until I saw the uncertainty growing in Kordo's eyes. His best efforts had been unable to pierce my defenses; his magic could not harm me. The more his confidence waned, the more mine waxed.

But in one last effort he rallied; I was forced to retreat, countering each of his desperate blows, waiting for my chance to finish it. I struck him only once more, but it was enough. I brought the Starblade down in an arc, dashing his sabers aside, slicing deeply into the side of his neck. He fell down dead at my feet, his blood soaking into the ground.

I had been right about his defeat turning the tide of battle. Giving a great howl of despair, our enemies fled immediately.

Led by Makrilda, the Malkins raced after them,

screaming in triumph without even a backward glance at me.

For a moment I almost followed, to add my strength to their attack. But then I thought better of it. I'd done enough here. Without my contribution they'd have lost, so let them finish it. I went back to collect my staff and bag, then headed first west and then south.

I intended to get clear of the Pendle district, though I had no specific destination in mind. I desperately wanted to find Alice, but I had no idea where to look. I hoped she would make contact again, but I couldn't rely on it. She'd gone off so suddenly. *Couldn't she have left a message for me with one of the witches?* I thought angrily. Her behavior did not bode well. Had she betrayed me? I wondered.

I decided to cross the River Ribble and head back toward Chipenden. And if there were enemies still lying in wait there, then it would be all the worse for them. It didn't matter how many there were—I'd make my approach down the ley line and feed them to Kratch.

As I walked, I could still hear booms and crashes from the direction of Burnley. I was now convinced that it was cannon fire. A battle was taking place. I'd been taking my time, but when a County storm came blustering out of the west, I picked up my pace.

When the light began to fail, I still hadn't crossed the

river. Still, I knew where I could shelter for the night. Nearby stood a ruined farmhouse, one I'd often used with my master. Only one wall was standing, but there was a cellar. It smelled musty, but at least it was dry and provided cover from the driving rain.

After lighting a candle, I settled down on the cold flags. I was exhausted and drifted off to sleep almost immediately.

I was awakened by a disturbing noise—as if someone was scratching on the wall with some tool, or perhaps with a claw.

I came to my feet cautiously and picked up the candle. Listening carefully, I quickly found the source of the sound: it came from high on the back wall. I saw that small spidery letters were appearing there, etched into the mossy stones. Was there someone or something in the cellar, invisible to me but writing on the wall?

I held the candle close and read.

Tom, this is Alice. I'll meet you at the Samlesbury Bridge east of Preston. Join me there just as soon as you can. We need to travel to Lukrasta's tower in Cymru.

I'd been waiting for a message from Alice, but I was annoyed by its content. Suddenly I wondered if it really *was* from her. Perhaps I was being lured into a trap.

"Can you hear me, Alice?" I demanded.

There was no reply. There was no water or mirror nearby, so she was probably using some other kind of magic to communicate with me. Maybe it only worked one way; it seemed there was no way for me to tell her what I thought.

When Alice had asked me to hurry to Malkin Tower, I'd been only too happy to do so. But she had gone off with Lukrasta before I'd even arrived. Now she expected me to make an even longer journey to a second tower—the one in Cymru. Was she playing games with me?

Two towers—that was one tower too many!

Alice was able to use the space between worlds, so I wondered why she couldn't come and talk to me here. And why did she want me to go to Cymru? Lukrasta was the last person I wanted to see.

One thing made up my mind for me. I'd spent several days with an exact replica of Bill Arkwright. It had looked like Arkwright, and it had talked like Arkwright. It had been totally convincing. Then Nora had proved to be a tulpa too—no doubt also a creation of Balkai. I wondered if this was happening again. I'd believed that Lukrasta was dead . . . but what if he *was* dead and had been replaced? What if he was a tulpa too? Alice might be in real danger.

I had to go and help her.

Soon I was striding down the Ribble Valley through the rain and the pitch black. I reached the Samlesbury Bridge just before noon. The rain had eased, but the low clouds promised more to come.

Alice was waiting on the eastern side of the bridge. She looked as beautiful as ever, dressed in green and brown, the colors she'd adopted since becoming an earth witch. But her expression was serious. I longed to fling my arms around her and hold her tight. However, I halted a couple of feet away and waited for her to speak, feeling wary. I was worried that she had betrayed me . . . though I was still full of love for her.

Suddenly she smiled at me, and a moment later she was in my arms. I'd expected sadness and commiserations. Didn't she know what had happened to Jenny?

"Do you know that Jenny's dead?" I asked her.

Her eyes widened in disbelief. "Dead? Oh, no, Tom! How did that happen? I've been trying to keep an eye on you by using my magic, but the last few hours have been really difficult and dangerous. I was distracted."

"She was poisoned by a water witch."

She hugged me even more tightly. "I'm so sorry, Tom. Poor Jenny."

"Had you been there, you might have been able to save her," I said bitterly.

"We were fighting off an attack. I would have been too late. I'm sorry, Tom," Alice said with a sigh.

"Mab's sister Beth is dead too. Those witches you sent down into the dungeons to help me were slaughtered by zanti. If you hadn't left so suddenly, you might have been able to help. I've traveled a long way, and by a roundabout route, to reach you," I told her, my voice bitter. "You've led me quite a dance. So tell me what's been happening. Why did you leave the tower with Lukrasta just before I got there? Couldn't you have waited?"

Alice didn't reply, and we ended our hug without our usual kiss.

"Let's talk as we go," she suggested. "We need to go to Cymru as soon as possible."

"Then why don't we just use the space between worlds?" I asked. "You did that when you left Malkin Tower with Lukrasta."

"Too dangerous, Tom. They almost caught us—I can't risk it again. Their mages are lurking there, hoping I'll do just that. They're ready for us. We'll just have to walk."

"But why are we going there anyway?" I wondered.

"For the very best of reasons, Tom. We can use that tower to destroy Talkus."

As we headed south, it started to rain again, and Alice began to tell me what had happened.

Grimalkin

27
The Kobalos God

The ghost of the Kobalos mage questioned by Tom and Jenny had spoken of "gates of fire," and soon, still in the form of a silver sphere, I came to the first of these. It shone brighter than the sun, although I felt no heat as I passed through its flames. In the form of a sphere, I had no eyelids to protect me, and my vision grew dark.

There were three gates in all. After going through the third, I raced on through the pitch black for what seemed like an age, wondering if it was true darkness or whether my vision had been destroyed. I lost all track of time—had I been trapped in the portal? Perhaps it was a circle; perhaps I would be stuck in this tunnel for all eternity . . . but at least the tentacled guardian had not followed me.

At last I emerged into dim light. Above was a purple sky, and I found myself floating over a circular plateau strewn with rocks, surrounded on all sides by high cliffs.

It seemed like an arid desert, though at its center was a lake that bubbled and steamed.

I drifted higher to get a better view—and noticed things moving around the perimeter of the lake. Were they skelt servants of Talkus? I floated closer to investigate. Yes, I was right: skelts were scuttling along the shore as if on patrol.

But where was Talkus? I wondered. Where was his lair?

Then it came to me. I remembered that skelts could tolerate boiling water, how they had once hidden themselves in the steaming water of a kulad, a Kobalos mage tower, before emerging to attack me. Talkus was hidden somewhere in the depths of that boiling lake.

In the form of an orb, I could pass through walls without harm. The gates of fire had not harmed me either. But could I dive below the simmering surface?

There was only one way to find out. I dropped down and entered the water without a splash.

It boiled and bubbled, forming a gray-and-white haze so that I could see nothing. I continued to sink deeper and deeper—and then, suddenly, the water became crystal clear.

Below me lay a wide rocky plain, but my destination was unmistakable: a large circular dark opening, similar to the entrance to the portal in the castle turret.

But here, instead of the four couches, four large skelt statues stood guard, gazing up and outward, bone tubes extended threateningly toward me and any other interloper who dared to approach the entrance.

For one moment I thought I saw them twitching, ready to attack, but it was merely a distortion of the water. Moments later I had passed beyond them and entered the dark tunnel—where, suddenly, water gave way to air. I looked back up at the surface that hung directly above me, not one drop falling. I could see myself reflected in it, an orb glittering like quicksilver.

I floated down until I came to an immense cavern: the lair of Talkus.

The Kobalos god was below me. To my surprise, I saw that he didn't resemble a skelt at all. He was roughly human in shape, but enormously broad and muscular. A line of razor-sharp bones protruding from the flesh ran the length of his spine, culminating in a long, thick tail tipped by a murderous-looking bone blade. Instead of skin, he was covered in purple scales, but it was his stature that surprised me the most. He was maybe four times the size of a man.

Talkus was sitting with his head in his huge clawed hands, leaning against the wall of the cavern. The situation was just as Lukrasta had described: the receptacle that housed the god's soul floated close to the smooth walls, a red, throbbing, irregular-shaped mass of tissue, purple veins snaking across its surface. It was attached to Talkus's belly by a long umbilical cord. Gradually he was absorbing the soul into his body. Soon it would fill him with power and greater consciousness . . . but the process was not yet complete. He needed the soul stuff that remained in that pouch. Without it, he would achieve only a fraction of his true potential.

I realized that Lukrasta was right: if I took the pouch, the god would be forced to follow me. I sank to the ground and shifted into my human shape, looking up at the huge figure. His eyes were closed; he didn't seem to know that I was there.

Then, as I approached, Talkus suddenly opened his eyes and glared at me, his face twisting in anger. He lurched up onto his knees and reached out toward me, as if to seize my head and crush my skull. For such a large entity he moved very fast.

But I was faster. I drew a blade, seized the thick cord, and cut through it very close to his belly. It spurted blood, and the god screamed, agony contorting his features. I held on to the fleshy tube, wrapping it around my hand as tightly as possible, then returned my blade to its scabbard.

As the furious god reached out for me again, I changed back into an orb. I had no idea whether I would be able to carry Talkus's bag—after all, I now had no hands to grasp it—but as I soared away, the fleshy receptacle came with me, the cord attached to the orb.

As I rose, I saw another orb falling toward me: my reflection. Then we collided, and I plunged up into the water. Seconds later I emerged from the lake and entered the portal. Somewhere ahead of me, I knew, was the demon guardian. Would it sense my approach and try to block my exit? Would Talkus give some kind of warning?

I sped through the three gates of fire, my vision darkening once more. Gradually my eyes cleared and I glanced back, but saw no evidence of pursuit. Perhaps Talkus was unable to follow me in humanoid shape—in which case I would be unable to lure him back to the tower. But even if I failed in that, I knew that I must have damaged him. I had the pouch that he needed so badly.

All at once I glimpsed the writhing tentacles of the guardian directly ahead. Eight baleful red eyes stared at me. But I was small and fast, and I soared past the scaly body, through the doorway, and was free—though now I realized that I'd be unable to escape through the stone wall of the tower: *I* could pass through, but the bag could not. Unless I could find an exit, I would be forced to leave it behind. Then I would have achieved nothing.

I floated down the stairway, dragging it behind me. To the side were narrow windows, just wide enough to fire an arrow through, but they were not wide enough for my needs.

At the bottom of the steps stood a door, where I changed back into my human shape, turning the handle with my free hand. To my surprise, it wasn't locked, but as I pulled it open, a Kobalos guard swung at me with his saber, eyes wide with fear.

I avoided his clumsy slash with ease and drove a long blade straight into his throat. His scream ended in a gurgle, and he slumped at my feet. Immediately I heard the thunder of approaching footsteps, but I was now free of the castle. A second later I was back in the form of a sphere, soaring aloft, searching for the beam of light from the cauldron. Still there was no sign of Talkus.

I floated down the beam until it became a tree-lined path. Now in my human shape, I walked along until I reached the crossroads. Thorne was standing behind the cauldron, and she waved to me as I approached.

"That's an ugly thing you're holding, Grimalkin!" she exclaimed as she stared at the purple-veined pouch, which was pulsing like a heart. The tube attached to it was slimy and hard to grip; blood dripped from the end.

I smiled grimly. "Within this sack of flesh is the soul stuff of Talkus. I must take it to Lukrasta's tower."

"You can't go yet," Thorne warned me. "The sun still hasn't set there."

I looked down the opposite path and saw that the top of the tower was bathed in the orange light of the setting sun, while its base was in shadow. Still, I wouldn't have long to wait.

"I'll walk along and go through at the earliest opportunity," I told Thorne as I passed the cauldron and set foot on the other path.

Tom Ward

28
The Silver Fingers

Alice had much to tell me.

Pan had insisted she work with Lukrasta again to implement his plan to destroy Talkus. It cut into my heart like a knife, but I understood that she'd had little choice in the matter: their combined strength was needed to combat the god.

"Grimalkin is going to help. She isn't trapped in the dark like other dead witches," Alice told me. "She can visit the Earth and strike at our enemies—but only during the hours of darkness."

I listened to this news in astonishment, but there were even more incredible things to discover.

"Grimalkin is going to steal a piece of Talkus's soul and take it to Lukrasta's tower in Cymru. The plan is that the god will follow her and be trapped there by the mage."

Things were coming to a head. If this could be achieved, it might well bring the war to an end. Without their god, the power of Kobalos mages would be much diminished.

But could a mage even as powerful as Lukrasta really do that? I wondered. Could he trap a god?

"What if Talkus can't be contained?" I asked as we strode through the driving rain, hurrying toward the tower.

"That's a risk we'll just have to take," Alice replied. "He won't have reached his full strength; he needs the soul stuff that Grimalkin has stolen. If he's desperate, it might make him reckless. When we've contained him, Lukrasta will move the tower into a different time and expel him there."

"Will he move to the past or the future?" I asked.

"The future is difficult because it's unstable," Alice explained. "As you know, it changes moment by moment. And even if we leave him there—what if he survives? He'd still be a threat as time carries us toward him. In hundreds or even thousands of years, our descendants might have to face him again. It *has* to be the unchanging past. If we can trap him there, his imprisonment will last until the end of the Earth itself. Lukrasta's plan is to drop him into the molten rocks that once covered the surface of this planet. Then he will either be immediately destroyed or trapped in the rock strata when it cools."

"Do you trust Lukrasta, Alice?" I asked, staring at her intently.

"Why shouldn't I? He wants the same things we do, Tom: the destruction of Talkus and the defeat of the Kobalos. We've got to work together on this. Otherwise, all human males will be slaughtered, the females taken into slavery. Yes, he does want to stop that—I'm sure of it."

"How can you be sure that it really *is* him? What if it's a tulpa like the angel you created?"

"That was mostly an illusion; we only saw it from a distance. I've stood right next to Lukrasta. I'd know if it wasn't him."

"Are you sure about that, Alice?" I asked. "You'd better hear what happened to us. Remember Bill Arkwright, who we thought had been killed in Greece? He came to Chipenden claiming he'd survived and wanted to work from the mill again. He was totally convincing. Jenny and I thought we were actually walking and talking with Bill Arkwright. You would have been fooled too, Alice. But he was a tulpa. He even taught Jenny how to fight with a staff!" I added.

"What happened?" Alice said, looking concerned.

"He wanted to get his hands on the Starblade," I told her. "Once he had it, he would have killed us both. The horrible thing was, the creature really thought it *was* Bill Arkwright. He didn't know he was going to kill us. Once it began to doubt its own identity, however, it was all over. I named it to its face as a tulpa, and it fell apart before our very eyes. Something similar happened when Jenny was being treated for the poisoning. A servant called Nora was supposedly trying to help her, but she proved to be a tulpa too. She thought she was Nora, but she killed people anyway—she almost got the Starblade away from me."

I looked around and saw that the rain was easing again, the clouds blowing away to the east.

Alice smoothed her wet hair back from her forehead. "It's worrying to hear that their mages can create something like that, but just supposing Lukrasta *is* a tulpa—why have him come up with a plan to hurt Talkus like this?" she asked me. "What possible purpose could that serve? It don't make any sense, Tom. I can see you've good reason to worry, but you can put those troublesome thoughts aside now. Trust me, Lukrasta isn't a tulpa. Pan certainly thinks he's dealing with Lukrasta. Could a tulpa fool a god? It ain't possible. Let's just concentrate on what needs to be done."

Hearing the certainty in Alice's voice allayed my concerns a little. Maybe my fears were groundless . . . though my instincts told me that something was wrong, and they'd rarely let me down.

We rested briefly before continuing south, crossing the Mersey and then skirting the walled city of Chester and fording the River Dee. Then we headed west into Cymru.

I suddenly felt sad. The last time I'd undertaken this journey, my master, John Gregory, had still been alive. It was on the way back to the County that I'd been surrounded by enemy witches and faced death. Grimalkin had saved me, but now she was dead too. One of them had been my master and friend; the other had been my ally—and yes, my friend too. Now they were both gone. I felt lonely and empty inside.

However, I'd learned that Grimalkin could leave the dark and visit the Earth, so maybe I'd see her again. That made me feel a little better.

A little before sunset on the second day after leaving Pendle, the tower finally came into view. I glanced at the ruined chapel on the hill to the east. Both buildings were sited on a ley line.

Last time I was here I'd fought witches on the steps

that led to the tower. I'd been totally outnumbered and would have been slain for sure, but as I was on the ley line, I had managed to summon the boggart, Kratch, which had become a vortex of fire and had killed every single witch. I remembered a tide of blood flowing down the outside steps, carrying with it the pointy shoes—all that remained of them.

I had no clue what would happen inside the tower now, but if necessary I'd summon the boggart again.

Alice and I picked up our pace. As we approached, I glanced up at the balcony where I'd once watched Lukrasta kissing her. There was nobody there now, and no lights showed in any of the windows. The place seemed deserted.

"Will Lukrasta be waiting for us inside?" I asked.

"If he's not, he'll soon show up," Alice replied.

I reached and felt for the hilt of the Starblade where it protruded from my shoulder scabbard, as if touching it for luck—though I knew it was more for reassurance, to confirm that it was still there. Without it I would be almost powerless against the dark magic that might be hurled at me.

Grimalkin was dead, but she had left me this sword as her legacy. It might yet prove to be the edge that enabled us to triumph over the Kobalos and their gods.

We reached the stone steps, and I realized that I'd been wrong in thinking that all that remained of the witches were their pointy shoes. Our feet crunched on small pieces of bone as we climbed.

I looked up and wondered what awaited us within the tower. Was Lukrasta an ally or an enemy? If he was an ally, his magic might help us to destroy Talkus, which would make our task far easier.

At the top of the steps, I paused and glanced back over my right shoulder, gazing at the hills and woods of Cymru with the sea sparkling in the distance. But I remembered seeing other views from that same vantage point. Lukrasta had the ability to move his tower through time. From here I had also gazed upon an arid landscape with a swollen red sun. We had been far in the future, close to the final days of the Earth's existence.

Then, passing through a door within the tower, I had entered one of many possible futures—one in which Chipenden village had been destroyed by the Kobalos and many of the inhabitants slain. That catastrophe had not come to pass; I had managed to warn the villagers of the attack and helped to protect them.

What would I see this time? I wondered. What was waiting for me beyond that door?

I drew the Starblade. I was taking no chances.

Alice stepped forward and tried the door. It swung open silently at her touch. She stepped inside and beckoned to me.

"Put that sword back in its scabbard, Tom," she said. "You won't be needing it for a while."

I followed her into a small room containing two couches and a table, the walls hung with tapestries. Plates of food were set out: cold meats, and fruits that I'd never seen before. They certainly hadn't been grown in the County or Cymru.

"Help yourself," Alice invited, "but you ain't got long. Grimalkin can only visit the Earth after dark. The sun goes down in about ten minutes; when she arrives, all hell is likely to break loose!"

So much depended on Grimalkin completing the difficult task she'd been set. Only then could we play our part.

Alice and I ate quickly. We were hungry; since crossing the Mersey, we had only eaten a few mouthfuls of crumbly cheese. Once we'd finished, Alice beckoned to me again. I followed her out of the room and along a short corridor. Ahead of us, steps led downward and upward: we went down, and I counted them as we descended—there were over two hundred—but at last we emerged into a vast cylindrical chamber that at first glance appeared similar to the subterranean part of Malkin Tower.

But while the inner walls of that tower were mossy, this stone was pristine, and the air was warm and dry; it was almost as if it had never been exposed to the elements. The wall torches shone brightly, showing that unlike the granite outside, the inside was limestone, like the pale spire of Priestown Cathedral. It gleamed in the torchlight.

And while inside Malkin Tower a spiral slope ran from top to bottom, here precipitous steps led directly down. We emerged onto a narrow walkway that skirted the inner wall. There was a safety rail, but it did little to assuage my fear of falling into the vast void below. I couldn't even see the bottom. At the center of the cylindrical space, directly opposite us, a large metal cage hung by a single chain. It gleamed like silver, its base level with the walkway, and it stood five or six times the height of a man.

"That's where we'll confine Talkus," Alice said, pointing. "It's made of a silver alloy, and we've woven our magic into it."

"Where's Lukrasta?" I asked her.

"Nearby, he is, Tom. As soon as we get the god in the cage, he'll be here to do his bit."

Suddenly Alice's eyes widened. She sniffed three

times. I knew that she was gathering information—searching for something. "Grimalkin is almost here!" she exclaimed.

No sooner had she spoken than the torches began to flicker. They didn't go out completely, but they faded to a dull red like the dying embers of a fire. The area was plunged into gloom, and the air felt distinctly chilly. Not only that: suddenly a more intense cold ran down my spine—that special warning that a seventh son of a seventh son receives when something from the dark draws near.

The approach of Grimalkin could have triggered that. After all, she was a dead witch assassin whose natural home was the dark. But the feeling was extremely powerful, greater than I had ever experienced before. Perhaps Talkus was in close pursuit.

There was a flash of silver, and suddenly an orb was floating in the air directly before the cage. It must have passed through the stone wall of the tower. Something dark was trailing behind it.

I'd hardly had time to take this in before the sphere entered the cage and instantly changed into the shape of Grimalkin. She was holding a slimy, blood-coated tube attached to a palpitating bag of purple-veined flesh about twice the size of a human head; no doubt this contained

Talkus's soul-stuff. She let it fall, and it landed on the base of the cage, still twitching.

I studied Grimalkin. She looked slightly different than the witch assassin I remembered. Her hair was black as midnight—far darker than it had ever been in life—and there were dark shadows around her eyes. But her body was still crisscrossed with leather straps and scabbards holding her blades, and when she opened her mouth to speak, I could see her deadly pointy teeth.

But instead of calling out a friendly greeting, she glared at us, her face livid with anger. "I cannot leave the cage! What have you done? Free me, Alice! Free me before it is too late! Talkus will be here at any moment!"

Once Grimalkin had deposited the pouch in the cage, she needed to get out quickly. Surely Alice wasn't preventing her escape? I thought.

I turned toward Alice, shocked, and instantly read the puzzlement and dismay in her expression.

"My magic isn't holding you there, Grimalkin! It's not my doing. Lukrasta! Lukrasta!" she cried. "What have you done?"

Instantly the mage appeared on the walkway directly opposite us. He looked up at the cage and smiled, his new silver hands glittering at his sides against the darkness of his gown. Then he pointed at Grimalkin. "Now

I will eliminate one who meddles even from beyond the grave!" he shouted.

"What harm has she done to you, Lukrasta? She's our ally!" Alice protested.

"I need only *one* ally," he said, "and that is you, Alice. Together we shall be as gods. Pan and Golgoth are both weak after their recent battle and will remain that way for decades. After we destroy Talkus, who will be able to stand up to us? The Fiend is no more, and the power of the remaining Old Gods is fading. But Grimalkin poses an immediate threat that must be snuffed out before she grows too strong. Already she's slain Hecate and usurped her power. I must put an end to her. Or rather, I will let Talkus do it for me!"

The chill running down my spine intensified, and then, suddenly, the tower began to shake. There was a low rumble, and the stones beneath our feet vibrated alarmingly.

Talkus was approaching.

Alice raised her hands above her head and pointed toward the silver cage, which shimmered, and then seemed to twist and flex. She grimaced with the effort as she desperately tried to free Grimalkin before the god arrived.

Lukrasta's face twisted with rage, and he began to run

along the walkway. Eyes fixed as she hurled magic against the cage, Alice didn't see him coming—but he held out his silver hands to throttle her.

I moved forward to intercept him on the narrow ledge, but I had to ease my way past Alice. I had the Starblade in my hand and would have attacked him, but he was too quick for me. In a second he'd pulled Alice toward him and put his silver fingers about her neck.

"Take three steps back, or I'll cut her throat!" he warned me.

29
The Silver Cage

I didn't move; I was calculating my chances of striking Lukrasta without harming Alice. Those metal fingers could slice through flesh like a knife through butter.

He had his left arm across her shoulders, holding her tight against his chest, the silver fingers at her throat. The mage was almost a head taller than Alice, and a cut to that head would finish it. But could I strike before he slit her throat? My hands started to shake as I weighed my chances of success.

"I thought Alice was going to be your ally!" I mocked, my voice heavy with sarcasm, desperately attempting to buy time. "All you care about is yourself."

"Three steps back! Do it now! I won't tell you again," Lukrasta repeated.

I tensed for the strike. It would need to be perfect. I knew that I had the speed and the skill to succeed, but even in his death throes, the mage might slay her.

I took three paces back, and he smiled.

"That's better," he said. "Now lay the sword down at your feet."

"Don't surrender the sword!" I heard Grimalkin shout from the cage.

I stared at Lukrasta, but continued to grip the Starblade tightly. Once I put it down, I'd be helpless against his magic. He would certainly kill me; he might kill Alice too, which would mean that I had achieved nothing.

"Do it!" he shouted angrily.

There was a sudden roar, as of rocks grinding together, and the tower shook to its foundations. A red orb passed through the wall and hovered directly before the silver cage. This was surely Talkus, with an orb far larger than Grimalkin's. Could it even fit inside the cage?

Grimalkin stood facing it, blades drawn. But what could she do against a god? I wondered.

As the red orb floated into the cage, it took on another shape; one that was very large and roughly human, though with a long, heavy tail ending in a curved blade, sharp bones along the spine, and a cladding of purple scales. I was surprised by Talkus's appearance. I'd expected him to resemble a giant skelt, with multiple legs and a bone tube.

Talkus lunged for Grimalkin with a clawed hand, but she evaded it and thrust back with a blade, opening up a long cut on his arm. No doubt those scales were tougher than skin, but they were no defense against the sharp knives of the witch assassin. Black blood dripped onto the floor of the cage.

Next Talkus tried to snatch up the purple-veined pouch, but Grimalkin was too quick for him. She kicked it out of his reach and took up a position in front of it. Once more she cut him, this time on the other arm, close to the wrist.

The god roared in pain and rushed at her, attempting to grab hold of her, but she was too agile. She slipped past him and sliced her blade across his ribs. He screamed in agony and attacked again, swinging his dangerous tail in a rapid arc toward her head.

I was transfixed by this struggle between Grimalkin and Talkus, but out of the corner of my eye, I was also watching Lukrasta and Alice. She was staring straight at me, while his attention was partly on the conflict within the silver cage.

Was this the time to strike at him? I wondered. Suddenly I made up my mind. He was distracted; I'd never get a better chance. He'd be dead before he knew it, dead before he could harm Alice. I took three steps forward, concentrated, and swung the sword at his head in an arc from left to right.

But the Starblade never made contact with its target—for Lukrasta and Alice had vanished.

My heart plunged into my boots. The mage could have taken Alice anywhere. I might never see her again.

Then I noticed that the cage was beginning to swing to and fro like a pendulum: Talkus's great bulk and weight blundered back and forth, his tail lashing against the silver bars as he attempted to reach Grimalkin.

To and fro went the cage, each swing bringing it closer to the walkway. I moved farther around the curve of the wall, a desperate plan beginning to take shape within my mind.

I realized that Grimalkin couldn't prevail against Talkus alone. I intended to try and help her: I needed her desperately now—for what hope did I have of finding Alice? Lukrasta could have taken her to the space between worlds, and from there they could have gone anywhere on Earth. But Grimalkin, who could enter from the dark at will, could surely find them. She was my only hope.

I sheathed the Starblade and climbed over the rail directly opposite the cage. It swung toward me, then away again. Each forward swing brought it a little nearer the rail. As it swung toward me again, I balanced myself, then launched myself into space.

I hit the cage hard, desperately scrabbling for a grip. My heart leaped into my mouth as I felt myself falling, but my hand found one of the vertical bars, and I clung to it. The cage was designed to hold Talkus, who was much larger than me, so at least I could put my legs through.

The god still faced Grimalkin, his back to me; I thought he had failed to notice that I was there.

I was wrong.

He turned, snarled—then launched himself at me. Just in time, I reached up, drew the Starblade from my shoulder scabbard, and plunged it into his chest.

I tried to withdraw it in order to stab him again, but to my dismay, no sooner had I pulled it out than Talkus took the blade in both huge hands. The sharp edges cut him to the bone and his blood began to flow, but still he held on. I could only use my left hand to grip the hilt of the Starblade; I needed my right to hold on to the cage.

Again and again Talkus butted his head against the bars, his fangs only inches from my face, his foul breath washing over me. He continued to tug at the sword; gradually it was being pulled out of my grasp.

Then, just as I was about to lose it, Grimalkin came at him from behind, plunging her daggers into his huge back. He released the sword and went after her again.

Evading his attack, she picked up the pouch, repeatedly slicing into it with her blade. Pieces of it fell through the bars, and a fine gray mist rose up from the debris and began to dissipate.

Suddenly I heard a strange sound—a collective dolorous groan that had no visible source. Could it be the despairing cry of Kobalos mages from the space between worlds, the mages who would appear in this tower were I to lose the Starblade? Perhaps they realized that Talkus's full power was now lost to them. Without his soul stuff, he would never reach his full potential.

Now Talkus was driven into a frenzy of violence. Instead of attacking Grimalkin, he vented his fury on the cage, battering it with his fists and tail, butting it with his head. The silver-alloy cage began to flex and distort, its pendulum movement becoming more extreme. At each swing its base crashed into the stones of the walkway.

I clung on desperately as each bone-jarring collision of metal and stone threatened to dislodge me. Then, from below, I felt a blast of heat and heard a bubbling roar.

I glanced down in alarm. Previously the base of the tower had been lost in darkness, but now I saw that it was a fiery red. A chaotic storm of molten rock churned and bubbled far below.

I realized that Lukrasta had used his magic to move the tower through time. The building was shielded by his power, but below us churned the fiery chaos of the distant past. We had traveled back to the earliest days of the world, to the time when it was a ball of molten rock.

Now the mage intended to let Talkus fall into the fires below. If they did not consume and destroy him immediately, the rock would eventually cool and solidify, binding him within its rigid embrace until such time as the Earth and all upon it were at an end.

But how would Lukrasta cause the cage to fall?

It hung by a single chain. That would be the point of weakness.

Talkus struck the cage again, and a section of it broke away and fell into the fiery abyss. Instantly Grimalkin shifted back into the shape of a silver orb and soared out through the gap.

Talkus's blow had damaged not only the cage, but also the magic that confined him there. Grimalkin had managed to take advantage of this, but the god was too large to escape through the same gap. Why didn't he shift his shape? I wondered.

I needed to make my own escape, but the movement of the cage was so wild that I couldn't balance and make a leap to safety. But then I saw Grimalkin standing on the walkway, back in her human form.

"Leap, and I will catch you!" she cried.

I sheathed the sword and prepared to do as she bade me, my heart in my mouth: the leap looked impossible, but it was my only chance.

The cage crashed into the stones at Grimalkin's feet, and as it swung back, I leaped toward her, aware of the molten rock that lay far below. I felt her cold arms wrap themselves around me, and then she released me, and I was standing safely on the walkway beside her.

The cage crashed back against the far wall. Talkus was still battering it, desperate to break free. Again it bashed against the walkway—but suddenly the chain from which it was suspended broke, or was snapped by the magical force emanating from Lukrasta.

Was he lurking nearby but invisible? I wondered.

For a moment the cage seemed to hover in the air. Then it plummeted.

As he fell into the abyss, the god let out a scream.

Finally the cage hit the red bubbling magma below, and there was a spurt of flame as it was engulfed.

Talkus was no longer a threat to us, and the human world was now safe—but I still had to rescue Alice.

I realized that my heart was pounding; I felt breathless and lightheaded. I tried to calm myself by taking deep, steady breaths until at last I was able to speak. Then I looked at Grimalkin.

"I owe you my life," I said to her. "But there is one thing more that I need to ask of you. Could you find Alice for me?"

"Stay within the tower," she replied. "I will see what I can do."

Immediately she shifted back into a silver orb and drifted through the wall. She was my only hope of ever seeing Alice again.

30
The Truth about Alice

I waited for Grimalkin's return impatiently, pacing up and down the walkway. Far below, the base of the tower was once more in darkness, and I realized that we had moved through time again—but to which point on the line that led from the past into the future? Lukrasta controlled it. To which era had he taken us now?

After a while I climbed the steps that led up from the subterranean part of the tower to the corridor. I walked along it to the room where we had eaten, and beyond that, to the outer doorway through which we had first entered.

I opened the door and looked out. It was still night, and a half-moon hung close to the horizon. By its light I could see the hills and woods of Cymru and the ruined chapel; in the distance lay the sea. The scene looked exactly as I remembered it. I felt sure that we'd returned to our own time.

The image of Lukrasta's fingers against Alice's throat kept replaying in my mind. Would I ever see her again? I wondered desperately. Now, it seemed, I would be traveling back to Chipenden alone.

When I turned, Grimalkin was standing behind me. There was a strange expression on her face—one that was impossible to read. Alarm filled me. What was wrong?

"Have you found Alice?" I asked.

"She is still here in the tower. She wants to speak to you. She says it may be for the last time," Grimalkin replied.

My heart thumped painfully at her words. "Is she still with Lukrasta?" I wondered.

"She appeared to be alone. Had I encountered Lukrasta, I would have done my utmost to kill him. Somehow we must put an end to one who would set himself up as a god to rule over others. Climb the inner stairs. Alice is in the room right at the top of the tower—the one with the balcony. But now I must ask you two questions. First, do you love Alice?"

"Yes," I replied. "I truly love her."

Grimalkin nodded. Once again I saw that unreadable expression on her face. "Do you trust Alice?" she asked me next.

This time I hesitated before replying. Yes, I certainly

loved Alice—that was beyond question—but I was not so sure that I fully trusted her. In the past, whenever she'd deceived me, it had been with good reason. Even the first time she'd gone off with Lukrasta, it had been beyond her control: Pan had demanded it. But the years I'd spent close to Alice had left me with a sense of unease.

"You are hesitant," said Grimalkin. "Think it over and make up your mind in your own good time. But I will give you one piece of advice: without trust, love cannot endure."

"What will you do, now that Talkus has been destroyed?" I asked.

"I think that now the Kobalos will retreat back to their city of Valkarky, but I will hound them all the way. I will also do what I can for the human women they hold as slaves. My work is not yet done."

With those words, she shifted back into a silver orb and floated away through the wall.

Thinking about what she'd said, I walked to the end of the corridor and began to climb the steps that led to the top of Lukrasta's tower. The door stood open, and I saw Alice waiting inside, standing at the foot of the bed she'd once shared with Lukrasta.

She smiled at me. "Talkus is no more, so it'll mean the end of the war against the Kobalos, Tom," she said.

"Their mages will have lost their power, they will."

"Where is Lukrasta?" I demanded. "We can't allow him to live. We've seen what he plans! He'll become a tyrannical god if he is allowed to. He's a threat to the County and the whole world beyond."

"Killing Lukrasta ain't going to be easy," Alice said. "Lend me the sword. Let me do it."

I stared at her in astonishment. If I gave her the Starblade, I'd be completely helpless against Lukrasta's magic.

I shook my head. "I can kill Lukrasta myself. I've already bested him in combat, and I can do it again."

"Can't kill him if you can't find him, Tom. Ain't going to show his face while you have that sword, is he? But give it to me, and he'll be here quick as a flash."

Grimalkin's question came back to me: did I truly have faith in Alice?

"What's wrong, Tom? Don't you trust me?" she asked, as if reading my thoughts.

The witch assassin had been right—for how could I claim to love Alice if I didn't trust her?

I drew the Starblade from my shoulder scabbard and held it out, hilt first. She took it with a smile, then stepped three paces backward, away from the bed.

Instantly Lukrasta appeared in the room, a satisfied expression on his face.

My heart sank into my boots.

"What a fool you are, boy, to trust a witch like Alice!" the mage cried, moving to her side and placing his right arm around her. "Alice and I are closer than you could ever imagine. As a mage and a witch, we belong together. You can't conceive of such a bond. She's deprived you of that weapon, as I instructed. Now she will slay you with your own sword."

Alice was staring at me intently, her eyes filled with anything but love.

"Now you know the truth about Alice!" Lukrasta gloated. "She is totally ruthless. She will do anything to protect herself. That always comes first. After that she will protect those she loves!"

He was right. I had been a fool. My master had also been right when he'd warned me never to trust a girl with pointy shoes, never to trust a witch. I should have listened to him. But I put those thoughts aside. I knew that everything was over for me, but somehow, even though things seemed hopeless, I couldn't give up. The training I'd received from John Gregory, my experiences as an apprentice and then a spook—they had taught me that while there was breath, there was hope.

Things could change at the very last moment.

I tried to take a step toward Lukrasta, but my feet wouldn't move. He was holding me in thrall, immobilizing me with his dark power. I fought against it—after all, I was a seventh son of a seventh son. But it was no good. Bringing all my will to bear, I still couldn't move.

"Kill him, Alice! Slay him with his sword!" Lukrasta commanded. "Do it now!"

Grim faced, she stepped into the space between the mage and me and pointed the sword at my throat.

I couldn't believe it. In desperation, I tried to use the gift that had saved me so often before: controlling the passage of time. However, I knew that my power had waned—though I saw Alice's eyes widen as she sensed me attempting to use it against her.

Immediately her face twisted in fury, and she pulled the Starblade up and away from my throat, coiling like a spring, holding the sword high, as if about to cut my head from my body.

But I didn't close my eyes. I wouldn't give her the satisfaction of seeing my fear. I locked my gaze with hers.

Then she uncoiled, and the blade whistled down through the air, heading for my neck . . . but at the very last moment, she took a step to the left.

The sword missed my throat by a whisker; I felt the cool air of its passing.

It did not miss the throat of Lukrasta.

The Starblade sliced his head clean from his body.

"You thought I was going to kill you, Tom, didn't you?"

I nodded. I was still in shock, my whole body trembling. A tide of crimson blood crept across the floor toward us. Alice was holding the sword, but now it was pointing down.

"It was the only way to be sure of killing him. You do see that, don't you, Tom? He wouldn't have shown his face while you had the sword. *He* was the fool to trust me, so confident that he held me in thrall. I told him I'd get the sword and then kill you. He believed me."

"That look in your eyes . . . ," I began, shuddering at the memory. "You really looked like you hated me and intended to kill me." I stared at her. Even now there was something terrifying about her—and it wasn't just because she was still holding the Starblade with which she had slain Lukrasta.

"Had to be convincing," Alice told me. "Had to make him believe, didn't I? But you didn't trust me, Tom. You didn't believe in the love we share. So you can go back to Chipenden alone."

Her words hurt me, but I couldn't deny that I'd had a moment of doubt about her. She was right. I hadn't fully trusted her.

Then, all at once, I was distracted by the Starblade. Alice was staring at it too. She lifted it up, balancing the blade between her hands, frowning.

Something was happening to it. I saw that it was twisting, cracking, breaking apart, rust flaking off. Then, before my eyes, it was reduced to dust that trickled through Alice's fingers.

The Starblade was gone.

"Did you do that with your magic, Alice?" I asked bitterly.

"There you go, blaming me again, Tom! Why would I want to destroy it?" she retorted.

"Grimalkin said it was indestructible. That it would grow stronger."

"Who knows what's happened, Tom, but it was certainly none of my doing. Maybe its job is done now that the threat from the Kobalos is over. Maybe it was destroyed because it came into contact with Lukrasta's blood. He was the most powerful human mage who ever walked the Earth. Could be that's the price for killing him—the end of the Starblade. Who knows?"

I bowed my head and stared at the floor. The pool of

blood was now just inches from Alice's pointy shoes. I'd been wrong to jump to conclusions; wrong to blame her once more. But before I could apologize, she spoke again.

"I ain't coming back to Chipenden with you, Tom. Need to think things through, I do. Not sure if we can be together anymore."

31
A Price to Be Paid

I traveled back to Chipenden slowly and sadly. I had a lot to think about.

I had never felt more alone. First I'd lost Jenny, and now I'd lost Alice. The house at Chipenden threatened to be a very lonely place.

On the first evening of my journey, just as the sun was going down, I took Jenny's notebook out of my bag and started to read through it.

Much of it was as I expected—jottings on creatures of the dark and accounts of her experiences and training. They differed from my own notes only in that they were more detailed and descriptive, and her handwriting was much neater. But one passage caught my eye. It was quite recent, written since our return to the County from Polyznia:

It's good to be home again. The longer I stay at Tom's Chipenden house, the more I grow to love it. I like the garden, even the parts where we bind boggarts and witches. Dealing with them is all part of the job—I'm determined to get used to all aspects of the dark and become brave and strong. I intend to become a good apprentice and then, one day, an even better spook. This is what I was born for. My life only began the day I was apprenticed to Tom Ward.

That last line brought tears to my eyes. All Jenny's efforts, all the training I'd given her, had just taken her step by step toward her own death.

I could console myself with only one thing: Jenny had been happy during her apprenticeship. I was going to miss her companionship—even the cheeky attitude that kept me on my toes.

It was hard to be a spook. It was a dangerous and lonely job. But one of the hardest things of all, I realized now, was training an apprentice, only to have that life snuffed out. More than a third of my master's apprentices had died during their training, so this was almost certain to happen to me again. It was a sobering and distressing thought.

Jenny had been brave and talented, and I didn't regret

taking her on. If the opportunity arose, I would certainly take on another girl.

In any case, I would need to find a new apprentice soon. The house up on Anglezarke Moor and the mill on the canal now both lacked spooks. From now on, I would be obliged to cover those extra territories.

If anything should happen to me—what then? Who would keep the County safe from the dark?

I needed to train those who would succeed me.

On the outskirts of Chester I rested for a couple of days, buying food from a talkative farmer and sleeping in his barn. He had news of the war. The town was buzzing with excitement, for the dark army of the Kobalos was no longer camped on the far coast of the northern sea.

They were falling back, long columns of warriors wending their way north, retreating toward Valkarky. Our own troops were also standing down from their state of high alert. The local regiment had returned to Chester.

It was commonly believed that our enemies had overextended themselves, that their supply lines were too long to sustain that vast army.

But I knew better. The truth was that the destruction of their god, Talkus, and the deaths of many of their ruling mages had undermined their will to wage war. As far as I knew, Balkai still lived, but whether or not the more benign factions within Kobalos society would manage to form a stable and peaceable regime in the future remained to be seen. There would probably always be conflict between humans and Kobalos, but that dark dream of world domination was over.

The danger had receded.

The County was safe.

I continued north at a leisurely pace.

It was a long time since I'd last washed. I was caked in dirt and my clothes and body stank. So when I spotted a small lake amid a copse of trees, I was tempted to bathe.

Though it was almost noon and there was a pleasant warmth from the sun, a lake like that would always be chilly, even at the height of summer. So I nearly kept going—but then I found myself tugging off my boots and socks.

First I washed my socks. I didn't bother with my gown—that could wait until I got back to Chipenden—but I did my best with my breeches and shirt; I wrung out the water, laid them out to dry on the bank, and then, after taking a deep breath, plunged into the lake.

It was icy—even colder than I'd expected. It sucked

the breath out of my body and almost stopped my heart. I didn't stay in for more than a minute.

When I emerged naked onto the bank, dripping with water, four armed Kobalos warriors were waiting for me. One had a shaved face, marking him as a mage; another had the three pigtails that told me he was a Shaiksa assassin.

My first thought was to summon Kratch, but I was at least three miles from the nearest ley line.

I didn't need to ask the name of the mage, but he told me anyway, looking me up and down contemptuously as he did so. "I find it hard to believe that a little human like you has caused so much trouble and inflicted so much death upon my people. My name is Balkai, and there is a price to be paid for what you have done. We will extract it slowly and painfully."

I suddenly realized that I'd become complacent, thinking that the threat from the Kobalos was over, assuming that because they'd lost their god and many of their mages, and were now retreating north, they would seek no retribution.

I'd been so focused on my rift with Alice that I hadn't given much thought to Balkai, the mage who had probably created the two tulpas.

But he had given a lot of thought to me.

He wanted revenge.

And I had no Starblade to protect me against his magic.

The two warriors had quickly moved behind me, and before I could speak, one of them delivered a punch to my kidneys with his mailed fist. I dropped to my knees in agony. Perhaps I lost consciousness for a moment, but then I felt myself being dragged across the ground; my limbs felt weak, and I was unable to move.

I heard the voice of Balkai again. "Dig it there!" he commanded, pointing to a spot a little way off.

I was lying motionless on my back, in thrall to his dark magic. The mage and the Shaiksa assassin stared down at me with pitiless faces.

"They are digging your grave," the assassin said, gloating.

"Do you know what the word therskold means?" Balkai demanded.

I remembered that it appeared in the glossary written by Nicholas Browne, but I couldn't have told him that even if I'd wanted to. I could hardly breathe, let alone speak.

"It is our name for a threshold upon which a word of interdiction or harming has been laid. Sometimes it simply guards a doorway, preventing access. In this case I have used it to seal this whole area, preventing anyone from entering or even detecting our presence. So do not expect to be rescued. Even the ravens who watch from the dark will not be able to find you. No one will intervene. We have all the time in the world in which to punish you."

I had no doubt that what Balkai said was true, yet I still hoped. Help might come from two directions; I had two chances of escaping with my life. I thought of Grimalkin, who would be busy hounding the retreating Kobalos army. I felt sure that if she knew of my plight, she would take time from that to help me. However, I recalled that she could only visit the Earth during the hours of darkness. The sun was still high in the sky; I could not expect her to appear before dusk.

Then I thought of Alice. Surely, despite our recent differences, she would try to help if she knew of my dire situation. Her magic was strong. She might be able to probe beyond the therskold and see what was happening to me. . . . It was a hope that I clung to.

Suddenly I found myself being dragged by my feet toward the hole that had been prepared for me, my head bumping along the ground. They flung me in. Deep in my grave, I was still unable to move, and it was still an effort to draw breath. Nevertheless, the Kobalos seemed to be taking no chances. Pegs were driven deep into the earth, and I was bound tightly by my wrists and ankles. Then they left me.

The sun was lower in the sky now, and I could no longer see my enemies—only the edges of the open grave and the sky above me. That might be the last sky I ever saw. I could see and smell smoke too. Nearby, the Kobalos had made a fire. The wood crackled as it burned.

Soon the mage and the Shaiksa reappeared and climbed down into the grave. The two warriors remained above, glaring at me. I saw that the assassin was holding what looked like a spear with a red tip, but I was finding it hard to focus.

All at once I realized that it was a thin stake with a smoldering point. The Shaiksa thrust it against my stomach, keeping up a steady, agonizing pressure, twisting it into my flesh. I tried not to cry out, but the pain was terrible, and I couldn't help letting a shrill scream.

The Shaiksa leaned on the stake with all his weight and I felt it pass straight through my body. He was making me suffer for as long as he possibly could. Then I lost consciousness.

When I opened my eyes, the assassin was still holding a stake, about to pierce my body. For a moment I thought that I had died and was reliving the moment over and over again. But then I saw the first stake still buried in my stomach. This stake was a second one.

"They say you are a seventh son of a seventh son,"

Balkai said, smiling down at me. "So it is only fitting that seven stakes such as this should pierce your body. Only after being transfixed by the seventh will you be allowed to die."

The Shaiksa touched the fiery tip of the second stake to my chest, high on the right; then he began to twist it into me. I smelled my burning flesh and screamed until my throat was raw.

They waited a long while before using the third stake. Looking up, I saw that the sky was darkening. The sun had gone down.

All at once I was filled with hope. Surely Grimalkin would come now, I thought.

The moon climbed high into the sky—I could see it from my grave—but still Grimalkin did not come. Gradually I realized that I was alone, and that I would die alone. Nobody would come to save me. I'd been abandoned.

The pain from the first two stakes was bad, but the third felt even more acute. I shuddered and convulsed in agony as the stake was driven through my left thigh. Somewhere close by, someone was crying and screaming and calling out to his mother.

Only slowly did I understand that it was me.

32
The Dark Assassin

I'd heard it said that in their death throes, especially in battle, men cry out for their mothers.

Now it was me—I just couldn't help myself. I was also begging for my life, pleading for mercy, whimpering, crying, screaming. The pain was unendurable.

The Kobalos were laughing at me, and Balkai spat in my face. "You are not so brave now, little human," he said. "A Kobalos warrior would not scream and beg as you do!"

They pierced me with the fourth stake, the fifth, and then the sixth. I was almost out of my mind with pain, screaming and raving. "Mam! Mam!" I called out into the night. "Help me! Help me!"

At first there was no reply. I fell into darkness again, and suddenly I was back in the kitchen at Brewer's Farm, where I'd been brought up. I was sitting on a stool by the fire, and I could hear the rocking chair moving to and fro: Mam was in the far corner, where the rays of the sun couldn't reach her. Bright light hurt her eyes.

Was I dying, my whole life flashing before my eyes? I wondered. Was this a vision of that time when, as a twelve-year-old boy, I'd asked Mam if I could stop my apprenticeship to John Gregory? I'd been so lonely and had found the job so difficult.

I remembered her reply: "You're the seventh son of a seventh son, and this is the job you were born to do." Then she'd said one more thing: "Someone has to stand against the dark. And you're the only one who can."

So then, reluctantly, I'd gone back and continued my training, hoping to make Mam proud of me. I'd fought the dark and won many victories, but it had been costly. Many people had died—my master, Bill Arkwright, and Jenny, to name but three. And now it had finally brought about my end too.

I stared at Mam, rocking to and fro in her old chair. She looked just as I remembered her—the kind woman who was the best midwife in the County and a good wife and mother. But as our eyes locked, I saw something relentless and fierce in her gaze, and I remembered her other aspect.

She'd been the first lamia; the mother of them all.

"What is it you want of me?" she demanded. Her voice was cold, and she'd stopped rocking, which was always a bad sign.

I suddenly realized that I wasn't reliving the past! I was actually face-to-face with Mam. She'd died triumphing over her demonic enemy, the Ordeen—though since then I'd once encountered her in something that was surely more than just a dream. Where she dwelt I had no idea, but I knew that somehow her spirit lived on. And now here I was, seeing her again.

"Mam! Mam! Is that really you?" I cried, my eyes filling with tears that ran down my cheeks.

"Yes, it is me, son. But don't waste your time crying. Tears never achieve anything. I'll ask you again—what do you want of me?"

"They're killing me, Mam. They're torturing and killing me. I've been abandoned. Please help me. I've nobody else to turn to."

"You sound like a child, son," she said, and she sounded disappointed. "You're a man now."

"I'm sorry, Mam, but the pain is so bad I'm almost out of my mind. I can't stand it. I can't bear it any longer."

Mam started to rock again, and the faintest of smiles spread across her face. "Until now you've done well, son. You've proved to be everything I hoped for. You truly have become the hunter of the dark. But I can't help you now, and the truth is, I wouldn't if I could. That's what a real mother does: she nurtures her children and then sends them out into the world where they must fend for themselves. You have to help yourself now."

"How, Mam? *How?*"

Mam was moving the chair faster and faster, the wooden rockers thunderous on the flagged floor. Now she really was beaming like the loving mother I remembered. "You are your father's son—a seventh son of a seventh son. But you are also *my* son, and *my* blood runs in your veins. So don't hold back anymore. Be what you need to be in order to save yourself."

With that, Mam and the kitchen faded from view and the pain returned . . . but this time it was different.

I could still feel the sharp, throbbing agony caused by the stakes that had been driven through my body, but now there was something else. I felt hot; there was a burning sensation inside me, like fire in my blood, molten rock running through my veins. I wondered if I was developing a fever.

I opened my eyes and struggled to see in the gloom. With difficulty, I counted the stakes. There were six: one in each arm and thigh, one in my chest and one in my belly. In the distance I could hear voices and more laughter. And I could smell smoke again.

They were preparing the seventh stake.

The sky above me was still dark, and cloud now obscured the moon. There was little light shining into my grave. I closed my eyes, thinking about what Mam had said. What did I need to be? And how could I become it? Soon I would simply be dead.

Was it a gift like the ability to slow time? I wondered.

Then I realized that there was something different inside me. With my eyes closed, I could visualize it in my head: something red, a glowing mass like a globule of blood simmering at the heart of a boiling cauldron, a sort of fire . . . I could feel it too.

The burning grew more and more painful now. It had spread from my body to my head; it was even worse than the agony caused by the stakes that transfixed me.

I groaned as my whole body was suddenly racked with fierce cramps. Arching my back seemed to ease the pain a little, but then I heard a snapping, clicking, cracking sound, followed by a sickening squelch. Ripples of pain ran up and down my body, which seemed to be contracting and stretching in turn.

The pain became more intense, and I screamed out loud.

In the distance I could hear the Kobalos laughing, no

doubt enjoying my pain. Then I fell into myself, down into the red core at the center of my being. It burned, but to my surprise the pain wasn't so bad there. It was a place of refuge.

I don't know how long I stayed there. It couldn't have been long, because the next thing I heard was Balkai talking to the Shaiksa. They were still by the fire—I knew that even though the edge of the grave shielded them from sight. I still had my eyes closed anyway. Their voices sounded very close, as if they were right next to me. They were talking in Losta, which I barely knew, yet now I could understand every word.

There was something else too: I could hear their hearts beating. Each Kobalos had two hearts, one in the chest and one in the throat—and I could clearly hear that double beat in each chest.

I realized that my senses had improved. Mam had been the first lamia, and her blood coursed through my veins.

"Be what you need to be." That's what she'd told me.

I was changing . . . was I changing into a lamia?

I listened, and found that every word the Kobalos said was crystal clear.

"Our armies must fall back to Valkarky, but it is not over. We can begin again. We can create a new god even more powerful than Talkus," Balkai told his warriors.

"My magic is powerful enough to do that."

Now, in addition to their heartbeats, I could hear the blood coursing through their veins.

I opened my eyes and saw that the inside of my grave was glowing with a red light. I could pick out every detail of my surroundings: tiny insects weaving patterns on the soil as they scuttled to and fro; worms moving deeper within it, creating labyrinthine tunnels. Above, the clouds still raced eastward, blown in by the wind from the sea. But I could see through those clouds to each of the myriad stars beyond. They glowed like eyes in the darkness.

There were smells too, odors sharper than I'd ever sensed before: the smell of grass, leaves, and the distant sea. But even stronger than that was the sweet odor of blood . . . though it wasn't *my* blood. For some reason I couldn't smell that, although I must have bled from my injuries. The blood I smelled was the blood of my enemies.

It was strangely attractive. It seemed to be calling to me.

I had no doubt now: I had changed into a lamia. It was time to take what I needed.

It seemed I'd been lying in the same place for far too long, so I sat up and stretched my limbs, freeing myself from the ropes. All at once I felt a series of irritating itches, and I plucked away the sharp stakes that had been driven through my flesh as if they were merely thorns.

I got to my knees and then my feet, luxuriating in the new sense of freedom. Why had I stayed in this pit for so long? Why had I delayed? I was strong and full of energy now.

I also felt a terrible thirst that only one thing could assuage: the blood of my enemies.

I bounded up onto the grass and began to move toward that delicious scent, toward the fire where the four figures stood. Two ran away at the very sight of me; the third charged toward me, jabbing at me with a pointed stick. I grabbed him by the shoulder, shook him, then flung him aside, watching his body turn over and over in the air before crashing into the ground.

The fourth, the larger one, was jabbering nonsense and gesturing with his hands. I reached out and ripped away the thin metal that clad his body. Then I drank his blood while he screamed in agony.

Later, still thirsty, I returned to the assassin. His neck was broken and his blood was almost cold, pooled by gravity within his body. I drank just a mouthful, then spat it out.

Next I searched for the other two, who were still

fleeing. I could have caught them, but the sun was rising and my need was diminishing.

Instead I walked toward the lake and knelt beside it, my mind empty. I stared at my reflection in the surface of the water. What I saw was not quite what I'd expected.

There were two types of lamia witch: the domestic and the feral. The former was almost totally human in appearance, whereas the wild version scuttled around on all fours, with sharp claws and teeth, and green and yellow scales. In addition there were feral vaengir, which could fly.

I certainly didn't have wings, but my reflection told me that my form lay somewhere between the feral and the domestic. I could walk upright, and as I gazed at my reflection, I saw that my face was still much more human than lamian. It was elongated and partly covered in green scales, but my eyes and nose were my own. My mouth was wider, and within it were two rows of sharp teeth almost as pointy as Grimalkin's.

I looked down at my hands. They were human in shape, but partly scaled, with long, sharp nails.

A domestic lamia retains its human shape because of close association with people; in isolation, it slowly turns toward the feral form—a change that can take weeks.

My transformation had taken less than an hour . . .

so, I reflected, I was different, something new; the result of both my father's and my mother's blood fusing within my veins.

Was the change permanent? I wondered. Would I stay like this?

All at once I felt utterly weary, my mind sluggish, so I lay down by the water, letting all my concerns drift away.

I think I slept for a while. When I awoke, I looked at my reflection again and saw that I had returned to my human shape.

I bathed, sluicing the blood from my body, then examined myself carefully. I could find no marks where the stakes had pierced me. Even the scales that had covered the wound I'd received from the Shaiksa I'd fought in Polyznia were gone. My skin was perfect, without a blemish. There were no calluses on my heels; my soles were as soft as those of a newborn baby. I'd have blisters before I'd even walked a mile.

I got dressed in clothes that were still damp, and tugged on my socks and boots. Then I put on my gown, picked up my staff and bag, and headed toward Chipenden.

As I walked, I thought about what had happened.

Was this a gift or a curse? Whatever it was, it had saved my life. I wondered if I could control this ability and use it in times of danger and need . . . or would it control me? I had become both more and less than human. With that first transformation, even my thinking had changed.

Yes, I was the seventh son of a seventh son—certainly the child of my father. But I was Mam's child too, and lamia blood ran through my veins.

I had always been worried about Alice succumbing to the dark. Now I had succumbed too.

Grimalkin was an assassin from the dark, but I was a type of dark assassin too.

There was a beast sleeping within me.

At last, just as the sun was going down, I came within sight of Chipenden, bypassing the village to climb up toward the house. It would be a lonely place without Jenny and Alice, I thought, but I'd just have to get used to it. I was the Chipenden Spook, and I'd certainly be kept busy fighting the dark. There'd be plenty to distract me from my sadness.

I crossed the garden, opened the back door, set down my bag, leaned my staff against the wall, and hung my cloak from a hook. I was hungry, but the only meal the boggart made was breakfast. So I headed for the kitchen, intending to make do with what I could find.

Even before I entered, I heard the loud purring. I

glanced inside and saw that a feast had been laid out on the table. There were meats and fruits and the delicious aroma of freshly baked bread. A fire blazed in the grate, filling the whole room with warmth and cheer. The purring was coming from the boggart, which sounded very happy indeed.

But it wasn't invisible. It had taken on its friendly, domestic shape and now resembled a large ginger tomcat.

It wasn't sitting on the hearthrug either.

It was sitting on Alice's knee.

Glossary of the Kobalos World

Original written by Nicholas Browne
Notes added by Tom Ward and Grimalkin

Anchiette: A burrowing mammal found in northern forests on the edge of the snow line. The Kobalos consider them a delicacy eaten raw. There is little meat on the creature, but the leg bones are chewed with relish.

Note: I tried eating the creatures (which are hardly bigger than mice) and I definitely prefer rabbit. However, they are numerous and easy to catch, and are best eaten in a stew. With the addition of the correct herbs, the meal is tolerable.—*Grimalkin*

Askana: The dwelling place of the Kobalos gods. Probably just another term for the dark.

Note: This is intriguing. Nicholas Browne could be right, but could it be that the Kobalos gods exist outside what we term the dark? Cuchulain dwelled within the

Hollow Hills, accessed from Ireland. That too was not directly within the dark.—*Tom Ward*

Baelic: The ordinary low tongue of the Kobalos people, used only in informal situations between family or to show friendship. The true language of the Kobalos is Losta, which is also spoken by humans who border their territory. For a stranger to speak to another Kobalos in Baelic implies warmth, but it is sometimes used before a "trade" is made.

Balkai: The first and most powerful of the three Kobalos high mages who formed the triumvirate after the slaying of the king, and who now rule Valkarky.

Note: We have not yet faced Balkai. It is a terrifying to think that his magic will be more powerful than that of Lenklewth, who came very close to defeating us. Only the Starblade can protect me.—*Tom Ward*

Berserkers: These are Kobalos warriors sworn to die in battle.

Bindos: Bindos is the Kobalos law that demands each citizen sell at least one purra in the slave markets every forty years. Failure to do so makes the perpetrator of the crime an outcast, shunned by his fellows.

Boska: This is the breath of a Kobalos mage, which can be used to induce sudden unconsciousness, paralysis, or terror within a human victim. The mage varies the effects of boska by altering the chemical composition of his breath. It is also sometimes used to change the mood of animals.

Note: This was used against me; it leached the strength from my body. But I was taken by surprise. It is wise to be on our guard against such a threat and not allow a haizda mage to get close. Perhaps a scarf worn across the mouth and nose would prove an effective defense. Or perhaps plugs of wax could be fitted into the nostrils.
—*Tom Ward*

Bychon: This is the Kobalos name for the spirit known in the County as a boggart.

Note: It will be interesting to discover whether these boggarts fall into the same categories we have in the County or whether there are new types there.
—*Tom Ward*

Chaal: A substance used by a haizda mage to control the responses of his human victim.

Cumular Mountains: A high mountain range that marks the northwestern boundary of the southern peninsula.

Dendar Mountains: The high mountain range about seventy leagues southwest of Valkarky. In its foothills is the large kulad known as Karpotha. More slaves are bought and sold here than in all the other fortresses put together.

Dexturai: Kobalos changelings that are born of human females. Such creatures, although totally human in appearance, are susceptible to the will of any Kobalos. They are extremely strong and hardy and have the ability to become great warriors.

Eblis: This is the foremost of the Shaiksa, the Kobalos brotherhood of assassins. He slayed the last king of Valkarky using a magical lance called the Kangadon. It is believed that he is over two thousand years old, and it is certain that he has never been bested in combat. The brotherhood refer to him by two other designations: He Who Cannot Be Defeated and He Who Can Never Die.

Note: Grimalkin told me that Eblis is dead. He was defeated by Slither and finally slain by Grimalkin. So the brotherhood was proved wrong to give him the above designations. He was defeated; he did die.

—*Tom Ward*

Erestaba: The Plain of Erestaba lies just north of the Shanna River, within the territory of the Kobalos.

Fittzanda Fissure: This is also known as the Great Fissure. It is an area of earthquakes and instability that marks the southern boundary of the Kobalos territories.

Note: The fissure is north of the Shanna River, but both have been described by Browne as boundaries between Kobalos and human lands. It is likely that the borders have changed many times over the long years of conflict.—*Grimalkin*

Galena Sea: The sea southeast of Combesarke. It lies between that kingdom and Pennade.

Gannar Glacier: The great ice floe whose source is the Cumular Mountains.

Ghanbala: The deciduous gum tree most favored as a dwelling by Kobalos haizda mages.

Ghanbalsam: A resinous material bled from a ghanbala tree by a haizda mage and used as a base for ointments such as chaal.

Haggenbrood: A warrior entity bred from the flesh of a human female. Its function is one of ritual combat. It has three selves that share a common mind; they are, to all intents and purposes, one creature.

Haizda: This is the territory of a haizda mage; here he hunts and farms the human beings he owns. He takes blood from them, and occasionally their souls.

Haizda mage: A rare type of Kobalos mage, who dwells in his own territory far from Valkarky and gathers wisdom from territory he has marked as his own.

Homunculus: A small creature bred from the purrai in the skleech pens. They often have several selves, which like the haggenbrood are controlled by a single mind. However, rather than being identical, each self has a specialized function, and only one of them is capable of speaking Losta.

Note: In Valkarky, I encountered the homunculus that was a servant to Slither. The one that could speak was like a small man, and it reported directly to the mage; another took the form of a rat and was used for espionage. I found it easy to control and subvert to my will. There was a third that was able to fly, but I did not see it. Such a creature could be used to gather information about us at long range. The three selves of the homunculus share one mind (as did the haggenbrood); thus, what it sees is instantly known back in Valkarky.—*Grimalkin*

Hubris: The sin of pride against the gods. The full wrath of the gods is likely to be directed against one who persists in this sin in the face of repeated warnings. The very act of becoming a mage is in itself an act of hubris, and few live to progress beyond the period of novitiate.

Hybuski: Hybuski (commonly known as hyb) are a special type of warrior created and employed in battle by the Kobalos. They are a hybrid of Kobalos and horse, but possess other attributes designed for combat. Their upper body is hairy and muscular, combining exceptional strength with speed. They are capable of ripping an opponent to pieces. Their hands are also specially adapted for fighting.

Kangadon: This is the Lance That Cannot Be Broken, also known as the King Slayer, a lance of power crafted by the Kobalos high mages—although some believe that it was forged by their blacksmith god, Olkie.

Note: Grimalkin told me that this lance was finally broken by Slither, the haizda mage with whom she formed a temporary alliance. He used one of the skelt blades, Bone Cutter, to do so.—*Tom Ward*

Karpotha: The kulad in the foothills of the Dendar Mountains that holds the largest purrai slave markets. Most are held early in the spring.

Kartuna: This kulad is beyond the Shanna River. I believe it to be the tower once visited by the haizda mage called Slither; he escaped after slaying the incumbent high mage, Nunc. I believe that the second most powerful mage in the present triumvirate has now taken up residence there, in preference to Valkarky. Many of his magical artifacts will be stored in that tower.
—*Grimalkin*

Note: Grimalkin was correct; Lenklewth had taken up residence there. When we went to investigate the kulad, he laid a trap for us. We were lucky to survive and did not manage to seize any of his magical artifacts. Though he is now dead, there is no doubt that another mage will rise to take his place.—*Tom Ward*

Kashilowa: The gatekeeper of Valkarky, who is responsible for either allowing or refusing admittance to the city. It is a huge creature with one thousand legs and was created by mage magic to carry out its function.

Kastarand: This is the word for the Kobalos holy war. They will wage it to rid the land of the humans, whom they believe to be the descendants of escaped slaves. It cannot begin until Talkus, the god of the Kobalos, is born.

Kirrhos: This is the tawny death that comes to victims of the haggenbrood.

Kobalos anatomy: A Kobalos has two hearts. The larger one is in the same approximate position as a human one. However, the second one is smaller, perhaps a quarter of the size, and lies near the base of the throat. If decapitation is not possible, both hearts must be pierced; otherwise, a dying Kobalos warrior will still be dangerous.—*Grimalkin*

Kulad: A defensive tower built by the Kobalos that marks strategic positions on the border of their territories. Others deeper within their territory are used as slave markets.

Note: A number of kulads are also controlled by high mages. They use these as dwellings; they are also used to store their magic and magical artifacts.—*Grimalkin*

League: The distance a galloping horse can cover in five minutes.

Lenklewth: The second of the three Kobalos high mages who form the triumvirate.

Note: Lenklewth is dead now. He was a powerful mage whose magic seemed even stronger than Grimalkin's. I defeated him with the help of the Starblade, and a vartek swallowed him whole.—*Tom Ward*

Losta: This is the language spoken by all who inhabit the southern peninsula. This includes the Kobalos, who claim that the language was stolen and degraded by mankind. The Kobalos version of Losta contains a lexicon almost one third larger than that used by humans, and perhaps gives some credence to their claims. It is certainly a linguistic anomaly that two distinct species should share a common language.

Note: The mage that I killed near Chipenden spoke the language of our own land, rather than Losta. Grimalkin says that the Kobalos mages have great linguistic skill and have made it their business to learn the languages of more distant lands in preparation for invading them.
—*Tom Ward*

Mages: There are many types of human mage; the same is also true of the Kobalos. But for an outsider, they are very difficult to describe and categorize. However, the highest rank is nominally that of a high mage. There is also one type, the haizda mage, that does not fit within that hierarchy, for these are outsiders who dwell in their own individual territories far from Valkarky. Their powers are hard to quantify.

Mandrake: Sometimes called mandragora, this is a root that resembles the human form and is sometimes used by a Kobalos mage to give focus to the power that dwells within his mind.

Meljann: The third of three Kobalos high mages who form the triumvirate.

Note: During my visit to Valkarky, I fought and slew Meljann in the plunder room when attempting to regain my property. I do not know who replaced him.
—*Grimalkin*

Northern kingdoms: This is the collective name sometimes given to the small kingdoms, such as Pwodente and Wayaland, which lie south of the Great Fissure. More usually it refers to all the kingdoms bordering Shallotte and Serwentia.

Note: I am surprised that Nicholas Browne does not mention Polyznia, the largest and most powerful of those principalities.
—*Grimalkin*

Novitiate: This is the first stage of the learning process undertaken by a haizda mage, which lasts approximately thirty years. The candidate studies under one of the older and most powerful mages. If the novitiate is completed satisfactorily, the mage must then go off alone to study and develop his craft.

Note: I believe that the haizda mage slain near Chipenden by Thomas Ward had only just begun his novitiate, which was fortunate indeed. If the haizda had been such as Slither, the one I encountered in Valkarky, he would have proved a much more deadly opponent. —*Grimalkin*

Olkie: This is the god of Kobalos blacksmiths. He has four arms and teeth made of brass. It is believed that he crafted the Kangadon, the magical lance that cannot be deflected from its target.

Oscher: A substance which can be used as emergency food for horses; made from oats, it has special chemical additives that can sustain a beast of burden for the duration of a long journey. Unfortunately, it results in a severe shortening of the animal's life.

Oussa: The elite guard that serves and defends the triumvirate; also used to guard parties of slaves taken from Valkarky to the kulads to be bought and sold.

Plunder room: This is the vault where members of the triumvirate store the items they have confiscated, by the power of magic, force of arms, or legal process. It is the most secure place in Valkarky.

Note: In order to retrieve the property that had been stolen from me, I successfully breached the defenses of this place, which Nicholas Browne describes above as "the most secure place in Valkarky." I did not find it difficult—but this may be accounted for by the fact that my abilities, both magical and martial, were unknown to the Kobalos. I will no doubt find their defenses will be much stronger the next time I venture into that city. Additionally, the birth of their god, Talkus, will at least triple the magical strength of the Kobalos mages. —*Grimalkin*

Polyznia: This is the largest and most prosperous of the northern principalities that border the Kobalos lands. Their army is small but well disciplined, and their archers and cavalry are first-class. They are ruled by a brave prince called Stanislaw.—*Grimalkin*

Purra (plural purrai): The term used to denote one of the female purebred stock of humans bred into slavery by the Kobalos. The term is also applicable to those females who dwell within a haizda.

Salamander: A fire dragon tulpa.

Shaiksa: This is the highest order of Kobalos assassins. If one is slain, the remainder of the brotherhood are honor bound to hunt down his killer.

Note: Grimalkin told me that at the moment of death, a Shaiksa assassin has the ability to send a thought message to his brethren, telling them of the manner of his death and who is responsible. Members of the order will then hunt down his killer.
—*Tom Ward*

Shakamure: The magecraft of haizda mages, which draws its power from the taking of human blood and the borrowing of souls.

Shanna River: The Shanna marks the old border between the northern human kingdoms and the territory of the Kobalos. Now Kobalos are often to be found south of this line. The treaty that agreed on this border has long been disregarded by both sides.

Note: Before the ritualistic challenge by the Shaiksa assassin, all bands of Kobalos warriors retreated to their own side of the river. We have yet to learn the reason for this. Much of Kobalos behavior still remains a mystery.—*Grimalkin*

Shudru: The Kobalos term for the harsh winter of the northern kingdoms.

Skaiium: The time when a haizda mage faces a dangerous softening of his predatory nature.

Skapien: A small secret group of Kobalos within Valkarky, who are opposed to the trade in purrai.

Note: In Polyznia, Jenny and I confronted Abuskai, who has links with the above group. Later we met Slither, who will be the link between the Skapien and humans. We hope to form an alliance with them in order to change the government of Valkarky, end slavery, and finish the war.
—*Tom Ward*

Skelt: This is a creature that lives near water and kills its victims by inserting its long snout into their bodies and draining their blood. The Kobalos believe it is the shape that their god Talkus will assume at his birth.

Skleech pens: Pens within Valkarky where the Kobalos keep human female slaves, using them for food or to breed other new species and hybrid forms to do their bidding.

Sklutch: This is a type of creature employed by the Kobalos as servants. Its specialty is cleaning the rapidly growing fungus from the walls and ceilings of the dwellings within Valkarky.

Skoya: The material of which Valkarky is constructed. It is formed within the bodies of whoskor.

Skulka: A poisonous water snake whose bite induces instant paralysis. It is much favored by Kobalos assassins, who use it to render their victims helpless before slaying them. After death, its toxins are impossible to detect in the victim's blood.

Slandata: This is what the high mage Lenklewth called the "shameful death." Reserved for rebellious purrai, it is designed to make them weep with pain. Many cuts are made with a poisonous blade. Even the shallowest cut causes agony—as I know to my cost.—*Tom Ward*

Slarinda: These are the females of the Kobalos. They have been extinct for more than three thousand years. They were murdered—slain by a cult of Kobalos males who hated women. Now Kobalos males are born of purrai, human females held prisoner in the skleech pens.

Talkus: The god of the Kobalos, who is not yet born. In form he will resemble the creature known as a skelt. Talkus means the God Who Is Yet to Be. He is sometimes also referred to as the Unborn.

Note: Talkus has yet to show himself. His powers are largely unknown, but already he has increased the magical power of the Kobalos mages. He may yet prove the biggest threat of all.—*Tom Ward*

Tantalingi: This is a method used by Kobalos mages to see into the future. The high mage Lenklewth claimed that it is superior to both the scrying of witches and the method used by the human mage Lukrasta.

Note: When the opportunity presents itself, I will

investigate this further. The future is not fixed; it changes with each decision made and each action taken. Thus all such methods of far-seeing are far less than perfect. I suspect that Lenklewth was merely being boastful. —*Grimalkin*

Targon: This is the name that Abuskai, the dead Kobalos mage, gave to the being that guards the doorways of fire leading to the domain of Talkus. Jenny encountered it in the attic in the tower, and it was extremely powerful and dangerous. By using salt and iron, she bought herself time to escape. I have no idea how such an entity might be destroyed.—*Tom Ward*

Therskold: A threshold upon which a word of interdiction or harming has been laid. This is a potent area of haizda strength, and it is dangerous—even for a human mage—to cross such a portal.

Note: When I examined the lair of the haizda mage near Chipenden, there was no barrier in place. This was no doubt because Tom Ward had already killed the mage. So I have yet to test the strength of such a defense. Whether or not the barriers that protected the plunder room were examples of therskold or something similar,

I do not know. However, they were of little hindrance.
—*Grimalkin*

Trade: Although the unit of currency is the valcon, many Kobalos, particularly haizda mages, rely on what they call "trade." This implies an exchange of goods or services, but it is much more than that. It is a question of honor, and each party must keep its word, even if to do so means death.

Triumvirate: The ruling body of Valkarky, composed of the three most powerful high mages in the city. It was first formed after the king of Valkarky was slain by Eblis, the Shaiksa assassin. It is essentially a dictatorship that uses ruthless means to hold on to power. Others are always waiting in the wings to replace the three mages.

Tulpa: A creature created within the mind of a mage and occasionally given form in the outer world.

Note: I have traveled extensively and probed into the esoteric arts of witches and mages, but this is a magical skill that I have never encountered before. Are Kobalos mages capable of this? If so, their creatures may be limited only by the extent of their imaginations.
—*Grimalkin*

Note: The winged being that spoke to the magowie and seemed to bring me back to life was a tulpa, created from the imagination of Alice.—*Tom Ward*

Ulska: A deadly but rare Kobalos poison that burns its victim from within. It is also excreted from glands at the base of the claws of the haggenbrood. It results in kirrhos, which is known as the tawny death.

Unktus: A minor Kobalos deity worshipped only by the lowest menials of the city. He is depicted with very small horns curving backward from the crown of his head.

Valkarky: The chief city of the Kobalos, which lies just within the Arctic Circle. Valkarky means the City of the Petrified Tree.

Vartek (plural varteki): The vartek was the most powerful of the three types of entity that I grew from the material found within the lair of the haizda mage. The fact that it can burrow through solid rock means that it could burst up out of the ground right in the midst of a human army, so that they scatter in terror. It has three bone-tipped tentacles, the ability to spit globules of acid that could burn flesh from bone, and fearsome teeth. It also has many legs and is capable of great speed. Although it is protected by black scales, its eyes and underbelly are vulnerable to blades. It is impossible to know what size a vartek could achieve once fully grown. It could be the most daunting of the battle entities that the Kobalos may deploy against us.—*Grimalkin*

Note: On the battlefield, the fully grown varteki were terrible to behold. Towering above the massed ranks of Kobalos warriors, tentacles writhing in the air, their breath formed clouds of steam above them. Fortunately, the Kobalos failed to deploy them correctly, and our gunners slaughtered many of them from afar. Had they burrowed under our army, all would have been lost. —*Tom Ward*

Whalakai: Known as a vision of what is, this is an instant of perception that comes to either a high mage or a haizda mage. It is an epiphany, or moment of revelation, when the totality of a situation, with all the complexities that have led to it, are known to him in a flash of insight. The Kobalos believe this is a vision given to the mage by Talkus, their God Who Is Yet to Be, its purpose being to facilitate the path to his birth.

Whoskor: This is the collective name for the creatures subservient to the Kobalos who are engaged in the never-ending task of extending the city of Valkarky. They have sixteen legs, eight of which also function as arms and are used to shape the skoya, the soft stone that they exude from their mouths.

Widdershins: A movement which is counterclockwise or against the sun. Seen as counter to the natural order of things, it is sometimes employed by a Kobalos mage to assert his will upon the cosmos. Filled with hubris, it holds within it great risk.

Zanti: These were the first of the creatures that Grimalkin studied after creating them from the samples in the haizda mage's tree lair back in Chipenden. Human in shape, they are extremely thin, with spindly scaled arms and legs. Their heads are covered in black scales rather than hair, and their eyes are positioned wide apart like those of a bird, which allows them to see ahead, to the side, and behind them.—*Tom Ward*

* * *